"The view is so much better close-up."

You're so much better close-up.

He sat back and draped his arm across the back of Tara's seat. He'd worked too hard to let a romance with Tara get in his way.

Still, he was all kinds of tempted. He couldn't take his eyes off her, even when she was distracted by the game and everything going on around them.

A chant of voices broke out, growing louder and louder. One word, over and over again. Tara looked up. She pointed at the mammoth television monitor nearest them and laughed. Grant followed her line of sight and there they were on-screen, just the two of them. They looked amazing together.

Before he knew what was happening, Tara's mouth was zeroing in on his. "We have to kiss."

"What?"

"We're on the kiss cam."

* * *

Once Forbidden, Twice Tempted by Karen Booth is part of The Sterling Wives series.

Dear Reader,

Thanks for picking up book one in The Sterling Wives trilogy, *Once Forbidden, Twice Tempted*!

The series starts when a wealthy, enigmatic man dies unexpectedly and leaves controlling interest of his company to his current wife, along with his two ex-wives. The three women are thrust into a partnership, but none of them are sure they can trust the others.

In *Once Forbidden, Twice Tempted*, Tara, the first wife, who is fiercely independent, is vying with her ex-husband's best friend, Grant, for ultimate control of Sterling Enterprises. Tara never banked on Grant having carried a torch for her for years. Their chemistry is off the charts, but the company is already on unstable ground. Will they connect or won't they? And what happens when the other wives find out? I can't wait for you to discover the answer!

I hope you enjoy *Once Forbidden, Twice Tempted* and continue to read the trilogy. In the meantime, drop me a line anytime at karen@karenbooth.net. I love hearing from readers!

Karen Booth

KAREN BOOTH

ONCE FORBIDDEN,
TWICE TEMPTED

PAPL
DISCARDED

HARLEQUIN
DESIRE

HARLEQUIN®

DESIRE™

Recycling programs for this product may not exist in your area.

ISBN-13: 978-1-335-20934-4

Once Forbidden, Twice Tempted

Copyright © 2020 by Karen Booth

This edition published by arrangement with Harlequin Books S.A.

For questions and comments about the quality of this book, please contact us at CustomerService@Harlequin.com.

Harlequin Enterprises ULC
22 Adelaide St. West, 40th Floor
Toronto, Ontario M5H 4E3, Canada
www.Harlequin.com

Printed in U.S.A.

Karen Booth is a Midwestern girl transplanted in the South, raised on '80s music and repeated readings of *Forever* by Judy Blume. When she takes a break from the art of romance, she's listening to music with her college-aged kids or sweet-talking her husband into making her a cocktail. Learn more about Karen at karenbooth.net.

Books by Karen Booth

Harlequin Desire

The Eden Empire

A Christmas Temptation
A Cinderella Seduction
A Bet with Benefits
A Christmas Rendezvous

Dynasties: Seven Sins

Forbidden Lust

The Sterling Wives

Once Forbidden, Twice Tempted

Visit her Author Profile page at Harlequin.com, or karenbooth.net, for more titles.

You can find Karen Booth on Facebook, along with other Harlequin Desire authors, at Facebook.com/harlequindesireauthors!

For my agent, Melissa Jeglinski, who never fails
to come up with the craziest good ideas.

One

The greatest joy of Tara Sterling's professional life was watching happy clients sign on the dotted line for a multimillion-dollar home.

"The family is over the moon about the house." That might have been the case, but today, this particular family wasn't on hand to complete the purchase. The Bakers were spring skiing in Aspen and had sent a woman from their escrow company as proxy. "They're so thankful you got it for them at such a good price."

"I'm happy to help." Tara waved off the compliment as her assistant gathered and reviewed the paperwork. "It's my job."

"Very well done. There were an awful lot of bidders on this property."

Tara smiled and nodded, thankful for this blip of appreciation. Even if it wasn't directly from the buyer, she'd always accept some gratitude. Tara worked incredibly hard for it—her reputation in San Diego real estate was that of miracle worker. She had a knack for hunting down dream homes, and the negotiation skills to get them at the right price. Reportedly, other agents hated having to face her. They whispered words like *ruthless*. Tara felt that was an unfair characterization. She saw herself as simply unwilling to lose. She'd already lost so much—her mother when she was only nine, her marriage seven years ago, and last year, her beloved father.

The death of her dad had been an especially crushing blow. He'd been her guiding light through childhood and adolescence, a presence so solid that it had been devastating to lose him. It had been fourteen months and she couldn't forget one of the last things he'd said to her—*Don't wait to be happy.* She hadn't realized it until that moment. She *wasn't* happy. Despite meeting new people every day, her world had somehow become smaller—more acquaintances, fewer true friends, and zero love life. Most men were intimidated by her success, and she was disappointed by their lack of vision. If she was ever going to find love again, she needed a trailblazer. A maverick, like her ex-husband, Johnathon Sterling. He had vision. He was passionate and exciting. Unfortunately, he also had a wandering eye and was easily bored. Their marriage had only lasted three years. Half of it had been thrilling; the other half made her feel as though she'd never measure up. At least not as a woman.

So she'd turned to her career for fulfillment, and for a while, it worked like gangbusters. She made piles of money. She took the beautiful home she and Johnathon had shared, and she'd given it a complete redo. She'd bought closets of designer clothes and leased a brand new Mercedes every year. She'd done her best to show the world that her divorce had not slowed her down. One man falling out of love with her did not define her. The only problem was very little of that was making her truly happy. And it hadn't dawned on her until her father passed away.

"If that's everything you need from me, I'll get out of your hair." The woman from the escrow company stood and extended her hand across the meeting-room table.

Tara rose to return the gesture when her sights were drawn to her phone, which lit up with a call from Grant Singleton. Luckily, she had her ringer on Mute. She'd let it go to voice mail. "I believe we're all set."

"Perfect. The Bakers will be so happy to hear that. So will their contractor. He's eager to get to work. He has an awful lot of it ahead of him."

Tara showed the woman to the door. "Getting started on the kitchen right away? I know they weren't happy with the size of the center island and were thinking of adding a pizza oven."

"Oh, no. They're leveling the whole thing."

"The entire kitchen?"

"The whole thing."

Oh.

"New construction," the woman continued. "They didn't see any point in trying to salvage what was there. Once you opened up the kitchen, you might as well tackle the dining room, and it only snowballs from there. I realize the seller did a lot of work on the property, but it's not quite to the Bakers' taste."

This was a common occurrence in the more expensive areas of San Diego County. The land was often worth more than the structure standing on it. But it still didn't strike Tara as any less wasteful to tear down a gorgeous home. "They told me they loved the house. We negotiated based on their personal plea that they wanted to raise their children there."

The woman shrugged. "They will raise their kids there. Just not in that exact house. Gotta get a good deal somehow, right?"

Tara dug her fingernails into the heels of her hands. This was the exact kind of frustration that made her question what she was doing. Money wasn't enough. How much satisfaction could she take in a job well done when clients turned around and bulldozed everything she'd found for them?

"I hope they're very happy," Tara said and bid her farewell. She had to let this go. Just like she'd done dozens of times.

As she turned back into the meeting room to grab

her phone, the screen lit up again. Another call from Grant. Grant was an old friend, and business partners with Tara's ex-husband, Johnathon. She and Grant spoke every now and then, but it was odd for him to call her twice in such a short span of time. She should answer.

"Grant, what's up? Is this a butt dial?" Tara could admit that the vision of Grant's butt crossed her mind. She'd never seen it in the flesh, but the man looked amazing in a pair of dress pants, or jeans when he wore them.

"Thank God you answered." Grant's normally deep voice was breathless and desperate. He was usually calm and always in control. But those few words hinted at trouble.

"What's wrong?"

"Johnathon had an accident. I'm at the hospital downtown. How fast can you get here?"

Tara's stomach sank nearly as fast as her pulse began racing. Adrenaline kicked in. She beelined for her office, cradling the phone between her ear and shoulder and grabbed her handbag. "I'm on my way. Twenty minutes if I don't hit any traffic."

"Hurry, Tara. It's serious."

She came to a halt. "This isn't a joke you two cooked up, is it?"

"No. Of course not. Just get over here. We might lose him."

Tara was back to running. "Lose him? What happened?"

"There's no time to explain. I have to go. Just get here." Grant hung up.

Tara raced down four flights of stairs in heels and sprinted across the parking lot to her Mercedes. The midday, early July sun was fierce as she fumbled for her sunglasses. She tried to ignore her heart's thunderous performance in the center of her chest. She fought back waves of nausea. She and Johnathon had been divorced for seven years, but she still loved him and cared about him deeply. Even though losing him had left her hollowed out in the end, they'd had a magnificent ride. She couldn't stand the thought of not having him in her life anymore. And if she was going to allow herself a purely selfish thought in a weak moment, she couldn't live through another personal loss.

But Johnathon was impossibly strong. If ever there was a fighter, it was him. "He'll be okay," she muttered to herself as she zigged and zagged her way through traffic. "He has to be."

Luckily, the hospital had a valet, and she zipped right up to the stand. Tara practically threw her keys at the attendant as she ran in through the sliding doors and up to the information desk to find out where Johnathon was. She rushed down the hall, breathing hard, which only made the antiseptic smell fill her nose more readily. These were not pleasant aromas. They made her think of losing her dad. And her mom. *No more hospitals.* She couldn't stand them.

There was a wait for the elevator, so she hiked up to the fifth floor, emerging from the stairwell, huffing and puffing. And duly disoriented. Where was she? This did not look like a surgical floor and it was miles from the ER. The nurses' station was off to the right, but she only got a few steps closer to it before a hand was on her elbow, pulling her back. She turned to see Grant. All color had drained from his handsome face, making the contrast between his skin and dark stubble so much starker. He opened his mouth to speak, but in that split second, Tara knew, deep down, what he was about to say.

"I'm so sorry. They couldn't save him."

No no no. This wasn't possible. Johnathon was larger than life. He couldn't simply die on a Tuesday with no warning. This made no sense. "What in the world happened? Was he driving too fast on the Pacific Coast Highway again? I told him a million times it was dangerous."

Grant shook his head and pinched the bridge of his nose. "It was a total freak accident. Line drive to the temple on the golf course. I guess he was still conscious in the ambulance, but he hemorrhaged."

Tara clasped her hand over her mouth, struggling to keep her balance. Johnathon was dead. It didn't seem fathomable. He was not only so young—only forty-one—but he despised golf. None of this was fair.

"Where is he?"

Grant gestured with a backward nod of his

head. "I had them bring him up to a private room. Miranda's with him right now. I didn't want her having to say her goodbye in the ER or even worse, down in the morgue."

"Who called you?"

"Miranda. She was at the country club, in the middle of a tennis lesson when it happened. She was able to ride with him to the hospital."

Miranda was Johnathon's third wife. She and Tara enjoyed a pleasant enough rapport. Miranda was a highly successful interior designer and had done some work for Tara, staging homes for sale. "This is awful. They've hardly been married a year."

Grant took Tara's hand and led her over to a small waiting room so they could sit. "That's the least of it." His face adopted an even more somber look, something that Tara would not have thought possible. "Miranda's pregnant and Johnathon didn't know. She had to tell him in the ambulance while he was dying. She'd been planning to surprise him with the news. Tonight."

A profound wave of sadness hit her. Johnathon had wanted a family for a very long time. Children had been one of the bigger issues that came between Tara and him. She'd wanted to wait, but she'd assumed they were going to have a lifetime together. "Oh, my God. A baby. And now he's gone."

"I know. I can't even believe the timing. It doesn't seem fair."

Tara felt as though they were all taking a master class in unfair. "Her only family is her brother."

"She's really going to need a lot of support. Help with the baby."

Tara's heart felt impossibly heavy. She and Miranda weren't close, but Tara knew what it was like to be on her own. Adrift. With no one to lean on but herself. "I'm happy to help. Whatever she needs."

"Even as Johnathon's ex-wife?"

Tara nodded emphatically, even as memories of her short and tumultuous marriage to Johnathon flashed before her. Happy days. Sad days. Crazy, inexplicable days. "We were never right for each other. He wanted kids right away. I wanted to get more established in my career. He was always trying to squeeze everything he could out of life and I was too busy being methodical."

"For two people who weren't right for each other, you certainly fell fast." Grant cleared his throat. It wasn't the first time he'd voiced his displeasure with the way Tara and Johnathon got together.

Tara had met Grant and Johnathon on the same night, at a mutual friend's birthday party, eleven years ago. It had been Grant who'd flirted with her all night, and Grant who'd asked her out. But it was also Grant who got called out of town for a family emergency the next day, and it was Johnathon who swooped in like a bird of prey, sweeping Tara off her feet. She'd always chalked it up to fate. And Grant never seemed to suffer. He'd had plenty of women in his life.

"I know. That was just the way he was. Everything moved like lightning. It was stupid, and we were young, but I don't regret it." She heard her own voice wobble. Reality was finally starting to settle in. Johnathon was gone. Her first love.

Grant pulled her into a tight embrace. "Of course you don't. He was an incredible man. An unbelievable best friend."

Tara settled her head on Grant's shoulder and allowed herself a few quiet tears. She didn't like to cry in front of other people. There'd been too many times in her life when doing that had made her feel weak and vulnerable. But this was different. This was Grant. One of her oldest and dearest friends. A man she'd had a crush on for a day or two before his best friend took center stage. "He was also a human tornado."

"He was indeed."

"What's going to happen to Sterling Enterprises?" Tara asked. Johnathon and Grant had built their real-estate-development firm into a true empire, but Tara had been there in the beginning. She'd thought she was a part of the team, but Johnathon eventually decided it was a bad idea for a husband and wife to work together. He'd pushed her to focus on selling real estate, rather than building. And so she had, because she loved him and he'd had a vision.

"Sterling will be fine."

"You're sure?" She was still holding on to Grant. She didn't want to leave the cocoon of his smell or the comfort of his embrace. Being in his arms right now was like a soft wool blanket on a cold fall day. Nothing like the rest of the hospital.

"There's a plan in place for me to step in as CEO. I just never thought we'd have to use it." Grant gently rubbed Tara's back. "I'll have to coordinate some things with Miranda, since she'll be majority owner now, but I'm guessing that between her own business and the baby on the way, she'll gladly let me steer the ship. I don't see any reason for her to do anything different."

Tara sat back and Grant took her hand again. "You're the one who's going to have to break it to the staff. And fast. Before the media finds out," he said.

He nodded, keeping his fingers wrapped around hers. "And there's a funeral to plan."

It was all so overwhelming. "That's going to be a lot for Miranda to deal with. I'm happy to help. Is there anything else I can do?"

"Someone's going to have to call Astrid. I supposed I'd better start making a list."

"Of course." Astrid was Johnathon's second wife, the Norwegian supermodel, the one Tara didn't like quite as well. Johnathon had married her mere months after his split from Tara, and Tara had always wondered if there had been some overlap between them. Still, Tara had managed to build some affinity with Astrid. It was part and parcel of being a real estate agent. She found a way to get along with everyone. "I'll do it. You have enough on your plate. I'm sure she'll be nothing but distraught."

"Thank you, Tara. I really appreciate that. Are you sure you're going to be okay?" He gazed at her with his deep brown eyes. They were filled with sincerity and compassion, just as they'd always been. He had a big heart.

A totally irrational part of Tara's brain wanted to escape into those eyes—surely nothing could hurt her there. "I will. I'll be okay. How about you?"

"I'm always okay. You know me. We'll get through this. I promise." He leaned closer and kissed her temple, stirring up an echo of the attraction that had been there between them the night they met.

Tara's eyes drifted shut as she soaked up his touch. It had been so long since a man had expressed something so tender toward her. But she could only enjoy it for an instant before the world around her intruded again.

"Max," Grant said.

Tara's eyes popped back open, confronted with Johnathon's longtime lawyer, Maxwell Hughes, who'd walked into the waiting area. He was an imposing man, towering and skinny with dark slicked-back hair, like the evil genius in a spy movie.

"We need to talk," Max stated coldly. "Is there a private meeting room?" He unsubtly slid Tara the side-eye, as if she was somehow in the way.

"I should go." Tara got up from her seat. She was

upset enough. She didn't need time in Max's presence. He'd been unbelievably cruel to her during her divorce from Johnathon. "I doubt Miranda wants to see me or talk to me right now anyway."

"Max, give me one minute." Grant ushered Tara out of the waiting room and over to the elevator. He pressed the button for the ground floor. "I'm so sorry about that. The guy clearly has no bedside manner."

"Tell me about it. What do you think he wants? Is this really the right time for a meeting?"

Grant frowned, seeming just as perplexed. "If he wants to talk to me, it must have to do with Sterling Enterprises. Hopefully just a formality with putting me in as CEO."

"Oh. Sure. That makes sense."

"I know. The timing stinks. But let's be honest, everything about this is horrible."

Two

The last time Grant had been in the church in sunny Point Loma, California, with its breathtaking view of the rocky coast and deep blue Pacific, it had been to stand up as best man for Johnathon. That day, Johnathon married his third wife, Miranda. Now, little more than a year later, Grant was here to bid farewell to his old friend.

Grant shifted in his front-row seat and patted Miranda's hand, although she didn't seem to warm to it. He'd been doing his best to comfort her for three days, ever since she called to tell him that Johnathon had taken a line drive to the head. Even then, Grant had been so sure that Johnathon would be fine. If Johnathon was anything, he was a survivor. He'd come from nothing and clawed his way to billions. Johnathon always came out on top.

But that hadn't been the case this time. Instead, Grant arrived at San Diego Memorial with only seconds to say goodbye. Meanwhile, a frantic Miranda wept at Johnathon's bedside, begging him to hold on. *You can't leave. I'm pregnant.* There was a baby on the way, a child who would never know their father. And a series of events had been triggered, but it wasn't quite what Grant had banked on. After his meeting with Max, Johnathon's personal attorney, Grant had learned that running Sterling Enterprises as its new CEO would require him dealing with all three Sterling wives. They still didn't know it, and Max had suggested they wait until a few days after the funeral to drop the bombshell. Grant was still formulating a plan for managing the aftermath, but for now, all he could do was nod at the poignant things the minister was saying.

"Johnathon was larger than life, instantly memorable and completely unforgettable. He had a heart as big as the Pacific Ocean he so loved to surf in. He was blessed in his life with three beautiful wives, all of whom are with us today. Our condolences to them as they come to terms with Johnathon's untimely death."

A deep sob came from the pew across the aisle. Grant didn't need to look to know that it was Astrid, wife number two, who'd arrived from Oslo, Norway, with absolutely no idea who Miranda was or that

Johnathon had ever remarried. Grant had been left to smooth that over, just as he'd done on countless occasions during his friendship with Johnathon. He could only guess what was going to happen when Astrid discovered that Miranda was pregnant with Johnathon's baby.

Grant felt a pang of guilt, realizing how much it angered him that Johnathon had never told Astrid the truth. Johnathon may have loved all three of his wives deeply, but he'd created plenty of trouble for them, too. Grant had witnessed both the good and the bad. He hated the things that Miranda and Astrid had gone through, but in Grant's eyes, the wife who'd been truly unappreciated was the first—Tara. Beautiful, stunning, tough-as-nails Tara.

She was seated only two people away from him. It was impossible to not steal the occasional glance at her, just like he'd been unable to keep his eyes off her the other day at the hospital. She was a singular beauty, with glossy blond hair, flawless and glowing skin, deep blue eyes and full lips colored a soft pink. He'd wanted to kiss them countless times, but Johnathon had always been clear, even after their divorce: Tara was off-limits.

Still, Grant would need to pull her into his orbit now. She was highly skilled at persuasion, which meant she could be a strong ally in helping him deal with Miranda and Astrid. But would she stay on his side? That was a big question. Certainly Tara had loved Johnathon immensely and would want Sterling

Enterprises to continue on in his name. But no one could have guessed that the succession plan Johnathon had put in place came with a caveat—one that stripped Grant of control. And now he had to get it back.

The congregants stood as the service came to an end, and Grant excused himself to step out into the aisle as one of six pallbearers. The other five were all employees of Sterling Enterprises, including Clay, Miranda's brother. Separating Johnathon and the business was impossible. They were coiled tightly around each other. Noticeable in his absence was Johnathon's only living family, his younger brother Andrew. Grant had hoped that Johnathon's death would be enough to make Andrew show up. But some rifts ran too deep.

As Grant lifted the casket with the other men, it was impossible to ignore the great weight that now sat on his shoulders. He had to be there for Miranda and the child who would never know their father. He had to care for Sterling Enterprises and keep the company flourishing. He must also be certain that Astrid had the support she needed to get through this difficult time. And he would have been lying if he said he didn't want the chance to be Tara's shoulder to cry on.

The other day at the hospital had only served as a strong reminder that his attraction to her had never gone away. Anything romantic between himself and Tara never would have happened when Johnathon was still walking the earth, but things were different now. Everything had changed. And it was time for Grant to be one of the rare few to move beyond the specter of Johnathon Sterling. Certainly in business. And quite possibly in the personal realm, as well.

Tara dutifully filed behind the other wives as Johnathon was carried from the church. Miranda was first to follow the casket, trailed by Astrid. Each was racked with sorrow, Miranda quietly weeping and Astrid so overcome she struggled to walk. The four-inch heels certainly weren't helping. Tara's place in the processional was last, the farthest removed from her ex. In that moment, she felt it was her job to keep it together. She would speak for all three wives by offering polite nods for the throng of guests wishing to share their condolences. The sea of acquaintances, close friends and perfect strangers said over and over again that they were sorry for her loss. It didn't make it any more real. Tara could hardly believe that Johnathon was dead. She kept expecting him to step out from behind a pillar and declare that it was all a joke.

Tara knew that coming to terms with this loss would not be easy. She must finally face the mix of good and bad feelings about Johnathon, everything she'd avoided reckoning with when they'd divorced. She was deeply saddened by this realization; it left a hole in her psyche, but she couldn't bring herself to shed more than a few tears right now. It didn't matter that this was the time to let it all out. She'd first learned it wasn't in her best interest to show her emotions when kids at school teased her for still crying months after her mother had died. Johnathon had taught her to be tough, as well. Not in words, so much as his actions. He could be sweet when she was down, but he adored strong, upbeat Tara, showering her with affection. Being strong got her what she wanted.

A ribbon of relief zipped through her when she finally stepped out into the blazing sun of the July day. It was a gorgeous summer day, in the midseventies with a light breeze. She was dying to get back to her house across the bay in Coronado, take off her heels and maybe go for a walk on the beach. Clear her head. Begin the process of moving on. But she couldn't leave without speaking to the other two wives.

"Miranda," Tara said, catching up with Johnathon's widow. "How are you doing? Is there anything I can help you with? Anything I can do?"

Miranda turned, hiding behind a dark pair of Jackie O sunglasses. Her ebony hair was back in an elegant twist, but the streaks of mascara on her cheeks showed the evidence of her grief. "How am I doing? My husband is dead." She hugged her Louis Vuitton handbag to her side like a life preserver.

Tara was a little taken aback by the response. She and Miranda had a friendship outside the fact that they'd fallen for the same man. "No. I know. Today is incredibly hard. I shouldn't have asked. It was stupid of me. I'm sorry."

Miranda's shoulders slumped in defeat. "No. I'm sorry. I'm a mess." She shot a quick glance over each shoulder, then pulled Tara closer. "I'm a big ball of hormones. I can't even begin to process the idea of raising this child on my own," she whispered.

"I take it you haven't told anyone."

"My brother Clay knows. You. Grant. A few of my close girlfriends. That's it. I don't want anyone else to know. Not yet. It's too much to deal with. And I really don't want Astrid to find out before she's back in Norway. Johnathon told me how hard they tried to have a baby. Plus, apparently, Johnathon didn't have the guts to tell her that I even existed, so there's that to deal with. I'm sure she hates me."

"Don't say that." It was the polite thing to say, but Tara could only imagine what Astrid might be feeling. She was the sort of woman who put her emotions front and center.

Miranda shook her head in dismay. "Right now, I just want to curl into a ball in my bed, go to sleep and wake up to a different reality."

Tara pulled her into a hug. Normally full of life, Miranda was frail right now. Her pain and emptiness radiated off her. "I'm sorry, Miranda. I'm so sorry."

She stiffened in Tara's arms. "Oh, crap. Astrid is coming this way. I can't deal with her. Nobody wants to see a cat fight at a funeral. Sorry." Miranda tore herself from Tara's embrace, turned on her heel and disappeared into the crowd.

Before Tara had a moment to prepare, Astrid was tugging on her arm.

"I don't know what he saw in her." Astrid's Norwegian accent was thicker now than the last time she and Tara had spoken. Astrid had moved back to Norway right after her divorce from Johnathon two years ago. Perhaps the time in her home country speaking her native language had erased the Southern California edge her voice had once had.

"Miranda's lovely," Tara said. "But you're the most beautiful woman at this funeral, so I don't see any reason to be jealous."

Indeed, Astrid was a true beauty, the sort of woman who wore no makeup and always looked like she was ready for the cover of a magazine. She had lustrous honey gold hair, and was tall and willowy; all clothes looked good on her. It would be easy to envy Astrid, but Tara didn't have it in her. She knew that Astrid had suffered great emotional scars from her marriage to Johnathon.

"I can't believe he married again. He never told me." Astrid's perfect lower lip was quivering.

Tara didn't have an explanation for that. She couldn't begin to imagine why Johnathon wouldn't have told her. Tara had been duly notified each time Johnathon remarried. He'd always framed it as the polite thing to do, although the perpetually-single Tara had felt as if he was only rubbing it in. Unsure of what she could say that would possibly make Astrid feel better, Tara pulled her into a hug. Apparently her role at this funeral was comforting the other wives. "What's done is done. He's gone and we all have to find a way to move on."

"I can't imagine letting it go. Ever."

Tara tried to not roll her eyes, releasing Astrid from the hug. "How long are you staying in San Diego?"

Astrid sniffled. "I still have my penthouse downtown. I plan to stay for a little while. We had a dreary spring at home. Plus, being here reminds me of Johnny. I feel closer to him."

A corner of Tara's mouth quirked up. Astrid was the only person who'd ever referred to Johnathon as Johnny. It did not suit the Johnathon she'd known, but perhaps he'd been different with Astrid. Johnathon was certainly a puzzle of a man. Looking for an exit from her conversation with Astrid, Tara took a quick survey of the crowd, and spotted Grant, his easy smile impossible to miss. She wanted at least a few words with him before she left.

"Astrid, do you have my cell number?"

She nodded. "I do."

"Good. Call me if you need anything. I'll check in with you later, okay?"

Astrid took Tara's hand. "I want to make sure you know that I understand why he loved you. You're wonderful. It's Miranda who makes me question his sanity."

Tara was not about to wade into these waters. "Take care of yourself, Astrid." She pecked her on the cheek then beelined over to Grant, and gripped his arm. "Can I steal you for a minute?"

"You can have me for a whole hour, if you want." The hint of flirtation in his voice was impossible to miss.

She led him to the shade of a large island oak tree. "You don't want to know what I could do to you in an hour."

Grant smiled and removed his sunglasses, a few tiny crinkles gathering at the corners of his warm brown eyes. He ran his hand through his thick chestnut hair, and pushed it back from his face. He'd neatly groomed his five-o'clock shadow for the service, but it didn't hide the sexy hints of salt and pepper along his jaw. Grant was the hunky boy next door, twenty years later, the sort of man who was comfortable with his good looks, but didn't feel the need to flaunt it. He didn't walk into a room thinking about the way the lines of his suit accented his broad shoulders. But every woman certainly took notice.

"You know, you threaten me with statements like that, but you never follow through. Why is that?" He punctuated his question with a sexy narrowing of his eyes.

"Johnathon would be horrified to know we're flirting at his funeral."

Grant shrugged. "He would've done the same thing if the roles had been reversed."

"That's absolutely true."

He reached for her hand, gathering her fingers and holding them tight. "How are you holding up?"

"I'm fine."

"Don't give me the Tara Sterling, real estate agent to the stars answer, okay? I want the Tara Sterling, woman I've known since before she married my best friend answer."

"I really am fine, but I think I'm still in shock. Ask me again in a week."

He drew a deep breath in through his nose, but didn't let go of her hand. "I hear you. I think I'm in the same boat."

"I think Astrid jumped straight to full-blown grief."

"I hate that Johnathon never told her that he'd re-married."

"It sucks, but had they been in close communication? She was in Norway, after all. It makes sense that Johnathon and I would talk. We were always running into each other at parties or restaurants."

"They were talking. For sure. He had his chance." He gently let go of his grip on her hand and Tara couldn't escape the tone of his voice. Grant knew all of Johnathon's secrets.

"You should probably keep that to yourself. Astrid's plenty mad as it is. She had some ugly things to say about Miranda." Tara planned to keep mum on the topic, too. She enjoyed having plausible deniability.

"Just like we need to keep the pregnancy under wraps."

"I need to write all of this down. I can't keep up."

Grant's eyes went wide. "I have one more for you."

"You do? Something bad?"

"I need you to keep this between us, okay? Just for a few more days."

"Yes. Of course." A shiver went down Tara's spine. She didn't like the sound of that at all.

"Johnathon split his shares of Sterling Enterprises between the three wives."

If it wasn't for the swift breeze that blew Tara's hair to the side, she would have thought the earth had stopped spinning on its axis. "What? Why?" This made no sense. Miranda was the obvious heir to that stake in the company. She was going to be so upset when she found out.

"He knew that you didn't quite get your fair share when you two split up. Sterling never would've taken off the way it did if you hadn't been there at the beginning."

That much was true, and she'd never really gotten over the way Johnathon had pushed her out. "Wow. So he actually acknowledged that."

"And Astrid was there for him when the company was growing so fast that he was hardly ever home. I think he always felt guilty about that. As for Miranda, that's fairly self-explanatory."

The wheels were starting to turn in Tara's head.

She'd been so eager for a chance to pivot to something new and more exciting. To build something, not merely sell it and cash in. Her father had told her to stop waiting to be happy. Was this her chance to do exactly that? "It's going to take me some time to sort out why he would do this." A new wave of sadness hit Tara, washing over her. There was a part of her that would always love Johnathon, faults and all. "Did you two talk about it?"

"We talked about everything. You know that."

"So you knew all along?"

"Not about this." Grant looked off in the distance, unknowingly flaunting his strong profile. "No. This, he kept from me."

"I'm sorry. That's not right."

He turned back to face her. "You don't need to apologize for him. I hope you know that by now."

"What happens next?"

"Max will call a meeting with all three wives. Which is why I'm telling you ahead of time. I need to know if you're going to be on my side."

Tara raised both eyebrows at him. What was he saying? "Your side?"

"You know how hard I've worked. Sterling Enterprises should be mine to run."

Now she was starting to see where this was going. Grant was going to make a play for her shares, and possibly those of the other wives. She wasn't about to commit to anything now. She needed time to think.

"You know I adore you." It was good to butter up a man.

"I don't actually know that."

"Well, I do. But I'm sorry. The only side I can promise to be on is my own."

Three

Grant had spent days trying to figure out how this meeting with the three wives would play out, and he couldn't imagine a best-case scenario, one in which they agreed to sell their shares of Sterling to him. His position was admittedly weakened by the fact that he would have to buy them out over time. A substantial chunk of money now, but he'd need time to raise the rest of the capital. He simply didn't have that much cash lying around. His considerable assets were tied up in investments. He'd had no way of knowing that Johnathon would die. There'd been zero time to plan.

Money aside, the personalities of the three wives were a huge X factor. Miranda was normally level-headed, but understandably distraught. With the pregnancy complicating things, there was no telling where her loyalties would lie. Astrid was vengeful and angry over the secrets Johnathon had kept from her, and those feelings would likely only become more intense once she found out about Miranda and Johnathon's baby on the way. Tara was her own wild card, even when she could certainly be counted on for smart and reasonable decisions.

Tara was his most likely ally, but he had a real weakness for her. If anyone was capable of persuading him to do something foolish, it was Tara. Many times over the years, Grant would run into her and find himself searching for reasons to forget about loyalty, if only for one night. Yes, he'd promised Johnathon that he'd never go there. He'd kept his word. But his best friend was no longer here.

Then there was the fact that Johnathon had essentially screwed him out of a chance at reasonable company control by dividing the Sterling shares between the wives. So how far did the promises they'd made to each other go, now that Johnathon was gone?

"Are we ready for this?" Grant paced back and forth in Max's sprawling office, lined with mahogany shelves stocked with law books. His hands were clammy. The back of his neck felt damp. There was no telling how this would go. *Badly* came to mind.

"I was ready days ago. You're the one who asked for a delay. And I only obliged you in that request because we've known each other for so long. The wives should have been notified about this right away. I should have told Miranda at the hospital that her husband pulled the rug out from under her."

"Her husband had just died, for God's sake. Is that really the lasting memory you wanted to plant in her head? That in this instance he shorted her on what was rightly hers?"

A knock came at the door. Max's personal assistant stepped inside. "Mr. Hughes, the Sterling wives have arrived."

"Thank you." Max rose from his seat and buttoned his suit jacket. "Show them in."

Grant stood back, not wanting to appear as the orchestrator of this meeting. This was Max's show, and as far as he was concerned, Max could take some of the heat for what the wives were about to be told. He was certainly paid well enough for it. Still, it was impossible to stay put when Tara was the first through the door. He reflexively propelled himself toward her. Perhaps it was the promise of her embrace, the chance to distract himself with her perfume.

"Tara. Looking gorgeous, as always," Grant said. It wasn't merely a requisite compliment. She looked so beautiful he could hardly think straight—exactly why he needed to keep her at arm's length.

"Thank you." Delivering a skeptical smile, she steered him into a corner. "I'm guessing you didn't tell Astrid and Miranda?" she muttered under her breath.

"I never intended to. That's Max's job. Not mine."

Her sights narrowed on him, seeming suspicious. "So why tell me at all? Why not make me wait?"

He didn't have a good explanation, other than the fact that he'd needed to unburden himself from the secret. The funeral had been overwhelming. "We've known each other for a long time. I couldn't keep it from you."

"What do you have up your sleeve, Grant?" she asked in a whisper. "Are you planning on disputing this part of Johnathon's will?"

"No. Of course not. I'll explain it all as soon as Max has said his piece. I promise you it's nothing bad. This is a windfall for you, right?"

"I certainly never expected anything from my ex-husband. Max made sure of that in the divorce." She cast a look over her shoulder.

"You're on my side, right?"

"Yeah. Sure." She surveyed the room. Astrid and Miranda were noticeably not speaking to each other. "In addition to being on my own side, of course."

That wasn't exactly the answer Grant had wanted. Now he had to hope that money would speak the loudest, and he could get what he wanted—primary control of Sterling Enterprises.

"Ladies, let's go ahead and get down to business," Max said. "Please. Have a seat."

Miranda and Astrid were already occupying two of the chairs in front of Max's desk. Tara took the third, which was in the middle. It was a fitting spot for her. Grant saw her as the bridge between everyone here. Astrid still wasn't speaking to him, as she had rightly figured out that he'd known all along that Johnathon had kept his new marriage a secret from her. But Astrid needed to fall in line at some point. Grant knew things about her relationship with Johnathon that he was certain she wanted kept private.

Grant didn't bother taking a chair, instead leaning against one of the bookcases near Max's desk. He stuffed his hands into his pockets, his pulse picking up again.

"So, as you three likely know, all of Johnathon's personal assets have been left to his wife, Miranda," Max began.

Astrid noticeably shifted in her seat. "Then why are we even here? Did you bring us here to insult us?"

Max peered at Miranda over the top of his reading glasses. "You're here because Johnathon's ownership of Sterling Enterprises was shifted into a separate trust after he and Miranda got engaged. He wanted his fifty-one percent stake of the company to be equally divided between the three of you."

Astrid gasped. Tara pressed her lips together tightly, but didn't say a word.

"Excuse me?" Miranda blurted. "How did I not know about this? How am I just finding out about this now?"

Grant had worried about this sort of reaction, but he kept his thoughts and emotions to himself.

Max held up both hands in an attempt to calm the

situation. "The business was already a separate entity when you married. It's in your prenuptial agreement that Johnathon's disbursement of his shares of the company were at his sole discretion."

"And he told me I was getting everything."

"Unless it's on paper, I know nothing about that. But I can tell you that he left a note, which he asked me to read."

Now it was Grant's turn to object. "Hold on. I didn't know about a letter."

Miranda pointed at him accusatorially. "But you knew about the rest of it?"

"Not until the day we lost Johnathon. I assumed it would all go to you, I would become CEO, and that we would simply move forward in a partnership between the two of us." He turned to Max. "You never told me there was a letter."

"I'm following Johnathon's wishes. He wanted this read to the wives. I didn't really see how it was your concern. Honestly, I'm not sure you should be in the room right now."

"Grant should stay," Tara said. "He was Johnathon's right hand. And he's still going to be CEO. Nothing will change that."

"This had better be good. That's my money. That percentage of the company is rightly mine." Miranda crossed her legs, and then her arms, in a huff.

Max pulled the letter from an envelope, unfolded it and began reading. "Dear Miranda, Astrid and Tara, I've asked Max to read this in order to explain my decision to leave my shares of Sterling Enterprises to the three of you. For Miranda, I realize this might come as a disappointment, but I believe that the fortune I have left behind will last far beyond your lifetime. I know I have provided well. As for Astrid and Tara, the truth is that Sterling never would have become what it is today without their help and support. They shared in some of my success during our marriages, but the company has really taken off since Astrid and I divorced. It only felt fair that everyone share in it. Miranda, you have my undying love and devotion, but I have never stopped caring for Astrid and Tara. They will be a part of me forever, as will you. I hope you can all understand that my heart led me to this decision. It might seem unusual, but it makes perfect sense to me. All my love, Johnathon."

Grant was doing his best to gauge the reaction of the wives, but it was a tough read. The room was eerily quiet. None of them was moving or uttering a peep.

"Leave it to Johnathon to make a big show of things from beyond the grave," Tara said, breaking the silence.

Miranda shook her head. "I can't believe he did this to me."

"It's not like you need the money," Astrid mumbled.

"It's not like it's any of your business," Miranda answered.

Grant had to intervene before this became even more contentious. He pushed back from the bookcase and approached the wives. "Astrid. Miranda. Tara. Please. Let me just try to help you all with this." He took a seat on the corner of Max's desk. "I think the reality here is that what's done is done. I don't like this any more than Miranda does, but none of that matters. It was Johnathon's decision to show his appreciation to Tara and Astrid, just as it was also his decision to put me in charge as CEO of the company."

He drew in a deep breath, knowing that years of hard work and his entire future were on the line here. Any one of these women could make a choice that could hamper his ability to seize control of Sterling. He had to forge ahead with his plea, even when it might not work. "My twenty percent stake of the company does not comprise a majority interest, nor do any of your individual stakes, which I believe, if my math is correct, work out to be approximately seventeen percent of the company for each of you. Since I am already slated to take over as CEO, I would like to propose a buyout of your shares. Enough to give me the same fifty-one percent that Johnathon owned. That will put me in a position to run the company exactly as he did."

"What makes you think I want to do that?" Miranda asked.

"Shush. I want to hear Grant's offer," Astrid interjected.

"Don't you dare shush me," Miranda shot back, delivering a harsh stare to Astrid, then turning her attention to Grant. "Maybe I want to run Sterling. It doesn't matter that Johnathon named you CEO. Maybe I want to buy out the other wives. It's about who owns the biggest piece of the pie."

Grant's heart was racing. Were his years of hard work about to go down the tubes? "Nothing has to be decided tonight."

"Grant's right." Tara slid him a look that suggested she might still be on his side. He clung to the idea. It was his only lifeline.

"We shouldn't make any decisions right now," she continued. "I think the wives and I need to have a meeting on our own. Talk over our own objectives and goals. And see how Sterling does or doesn't play a role in that."

It was a perfectly sensible step forward. So why did it make Grant so damn nervous? Oh, right. Because she was suggesting a scenario in which he had zero control.

Miranda cleared her throat. "Fine. I can live with that."

"Me, too," added Astrid. "I'm not rushing back to Norway any time soon."

"Good, then. The three of us will meet tomorrow night. Is my house okay? Seven o'clock?" Tara asked.

"Yes," Miranda agreed while Astrid nodded.

"And in the meantime, Grant, can you present us with an offer so we know what we're working with?"

Tara's sights met his and he struggled to figure out whether his previous conclusion that she was on his side was indeed accurate. No wonder she was such a shark in negotiations. She did an excellent job of keeping her cool and remaining above the fray. He wished he didn't find this quality so appealing. It might eventually sink him.

"An offer as in one? Are you three negotiating together?" He hadn't expected the wives would form a coalition.

Tara glanced first at Miranda and then at Astrid. With a nod, they each agreed with her. Then she returned her sights to Grant. "Well, yes. I think so. It only makes sense. No need to hire three lawyers. It's not like I don't work on deals all day long. Or Miranda for that matter."

"I know what I'm doing, too," Astrid said.

"Of course you do." Tara picked up her purse. "I think that's all for now. I'll see you both at my house tomorrow night." Miranda and Astrid both made a break for the door, with Tara bringing up the rear.

"I'd like to ask for one thing." Grant was desperate to end this meeting with some input. "Can I make the offer in person? Maybe kick off your meeting tomorrow?"

Tara smiled wide at him, but it wasn't a warm gesture. "Grant. I see what you're doing. You know very well that it's harder to tell someone no in person."

"I think Johnathon would prefer it that way. I don't want this to become contentious."

"How about a compromise?" she countered. "Email us the offer, Miranda and Astrid and I will meet, then you can come over when we're done and we'll give you our answer in person."

Grant wasn't much for compromises. He'd had to make too many of them when Johnathon was at the helm of Sterling. This was supposed to be his time to take charge and make decisions. Damn Johnathon and this decision he'd made to split majority interest of the company. Why couldn't he have talked to Grant about it? *Eyes on the prize.* He had to deal with the circumstances right in front of his face—three women who held what he desperately wanted. "Yes. Of course."

Miranda and Astrid departed, but Grant had to make one last plea, so he grabbed Tara just outside the door. "Tara. We've known each other for so long. Please don't treat me like I'm the bad guy."

Tara hooked her purse on her arm and looked him right in the eye. "Grant. Please. You have stunning puppy-dog eyes, but you won't get my pity."

For an instant, he was too distracted by her comment about his appearance to think straight. "I'm not asking for that. You and the wives have my entire future in your hands and I'd like to know that I'm not going to get screwed over."

She kissed him on the cheek, leaving him to grapple with the resulting wave of warmth through his body. "You're handsome and rich. No matter what life hands you, I'm guessing you'll be just fine."

Four

Tara hardly slept at all the night of the meeting at Max's office, her head swirling with ideas. She'd gone in unsure of Grant's plan, thinking he might merely be trying to keep the peace. As CEO, he needed the full confidence of a solid core of shareholders. She'd thought he might work on building an alliance. Instead, he was trying to divide and conquer.

Which got Tara thinking about a coalition of her own. An unlikely one, for sure, but one that might free her from the shackles of her current career and let her pivot to something new. One where she could step in at a high level, determine her own destiny and bring her history with Sterling Enterprises full circle. She'd been there on Day One and unfairly spun out before things got good. It was only right that she'd step in after Johnathon's death and make sure the company continued to thrive. Perhaps this new direction would bring her some of that elusive happiness, exactly what her dad had told her to stop waiting for.

Leaving a late-afternoon home showing, she took the bridge over the bay into Coronado. She always felt more relaxed once she was on the island. It had always been too quiet for Johnathon. He preferred the hustle and bustle of downtown San Diego, which was where he and Astrid had lived together, or the slightly showier homes up on the cliffs in La Jolla, where he'd lived with Miranda. As for Tara, Coronado had the charm of a small town, with very expensive underpinnings. You couldn't buy a piece of property for less than two million and that was for a postage-stamp lot. Her home, a three-bedroom, three-bath beauty several blocks down Ocean Boulevard from the Hotel del Coronado, provided a stunning view of the Pacific while still affording her some privacy. It was the one thing in her life that gave her any peace.

Tonight, there was no telling if serenity and decorum would prevail once Miranda and Astrid were back in the same room. It wasn't difficult to envision a real dustup between those two. They had every reason to not like each other. But in Tara's experience, money did a lot to assuage hurt feelings. The the promise of a big payday might be enough to persuade them both to set aside their differences. Or at least forget about them.

Astrid arrived first, shortly after seven that evening, wearing black from head to toe in the form of a sleek pencil skirt, matching jacket and patent Louboutins. Either Tara was misreading the outfit or Astrid was trying to send the message that she was just as much a grieving widow as Miranda. Tara prayed Miranda wouldn't notice, but it was hard to imagine that she wouldn't pick up on it. Not that Tara had much time to think about it at all—Miranda came walking up the sidewalk less than a minute later.

"Come on in," Tara said, then closed the door behind them. She led them upstairs to the top floor, which was where the kitchen, great room and master suite were located. The ocean views were most stunning up there, on full display through a near-one-eighty degrees of plateglass windows. "Can I offer either of you something to drink? Wine? Sparkling water?" She knew she needed something nonalcoholic on hand for Miranda.

"Water is good for me," Miranda said just as quickly as Tara had thought it.

"I need wine," Astrid said. "I'll call a car if necessary."

Tara poured them each their beverage of choice, and reminded herself that she'd dealt with plenty of prickly situations in her real estate career. She could sell them on her plan. She mostly convinced herself.

"Let's get comfortable in the living room so we can talk about Grant's offer." She led them over to the seating area, complete with two large white linen sectionals with a chunky oak coffee table between. Her decor was beach-y, but elegant. Perfect as far as Tara was concerned.

"Can we call it that?" Astrid asked. "He's only offering to buy our shares in small chunks over the next several years. I'm not selling my shares to him. I would rather have my money now."

"You mean the shares of Sterling Enterprises neither of you should own?" Miranda asked.

"Let's back up here for a minute. There's no reason to get upset," Tara started, wanting to keep things civil.

"Upset?" Miranda cut her off. "That doesn't even begin to capture the range of emotions I'm feeling. I shouldn't have to be here right now, having this meeting. I shouldn't have to think about this. I feel betrayed by my dead husband. I feel betrayed by the father of my child." Miranda closed her eyes and pressed her hand to her lower belly.

Oh, no. Tara's sights flew to Astrid's face, anxious to gauge her reaction to the news Tara had been hoping wouldn't come out during this meeting.

Astrid's skin went impossibly pale and ashen. "Child?" she asked, her voice so fragile it was like glass.

Miranda's eyes popped open. It was obvious from her expression that she realized her mistake. She'd just given up the secret she'd wanted to keep from Astrid, at least until she returned to Norway. "Yes." She swallowed hard. "I'm about eight weeks along. It's early days."

Tara sat frozen, bracing for Astrid to explode. Miranda seemed to be doing the same. Neither did so much as blink or dare to utter a single syllable.

But Astrid did something no one ever could have expected. She smiled. "Johnny had a baby on the way?" A tear rolled down her high cheekbone. "He wanted children so badly. So badly."

Tara couldn't believe what she was hearing. Was that happiness in Astrid's voice?

"I'm very pleased for you. Congratulations." The look in Astrid's eyes was unmistakable. She still loved Johnathon.

"Thank you." Miranda blew out a breath. "To be honest, I thought you would be upset. He told me that you'd had trouble conceiving."

Astrid nodded, but she was pursing her lips tightly, as if she was holding back serious tears. "I can't talk about it. So please, let's just get back to business."

Tara's heart went out to Astrid. She was bearing a terrible burden. "It seems like none of us is particularly pleased with Grant's offer. And I've been thinking about it and there has to be a reason Johnathon did this. Something beyond feeling as though he owed a debt to Astrid and me. Maybe it was his way of trying to bring us together."

Astrid let out a breathy laugh. "One of us didn't know one of the other wives even existed. Why would he want to do that?"

Tara pinched the bridge of her nose and prayed for strength. Apparently going with a more heartfelt approach was not going to work. "Okay, then let's look at the financial side. Our shares are valuable right now, but they could be worth more later. And it gives us control no one else has."

"We each own seventeen percent. Grant owns twenty. That's not control," Miranda said.

"When our shares are combined, we have Johnathon's majority interest. Fifty-one percent. We could run the company. Together."

"But Grant has been named as CEO. Where does that leave us?" Miranda countered.

"He could still be CEO. It would just be the three of us as a single voting bloc, making decisions about the direction of the company. And filling vacancies. There are senior management positions and spots on the acquisitions team."

"I don't need a job," Miranda said. "My interior design business is booming and I have more than enough money. Johnathon did manage to leave everything else to me."

Tara realized Miranda was making a valid point. "You wouldn't have to take a position at Sterling. The key is voting together. Sticking together."

"I think I would want a job," Astrid offered. "I can't sit around my apartment all day long."

"You've decided to stay in San Diego?" Tara asked.

Astrid shrugged. "If I had a reason, I could stay. At least for a while."

"I'm still not sold on this idea," Miranda said. "Maybe we should let Grant slowly buy us out. It's not like he doesn't deserve it. He's worked plenty hard."

"This isn't about taking anything away from Grant." Tara could feel her frustration growing. She really wanted them to see that this was a fantastic opportunity. "Let's think about what we're leaving for Johnathon's child. Houses and money are great, but wouldn't it be nice to hand off an actual legacy? This was Johnathon's passion and it was immensely important to him. The baby should at least have a chance at that when he or she is grown. If you sell your shares, the baby won't have any piece of the company."

The room fell incredibly quiet. Astrid was staring at Miranda, while Miranda peered down at her belly. She had no baby pooch yet, but it wouldn't be long until it was there. Tara hoped that all of this quiet meant that her plea had been effective. But she also realized how much weight it gave to the situation. There was a baby on the way, and although he or she would always have money, they would never know their dad. All three of them were standing in the midst of tragedy, with Tara trying to get them to look beyond it. See the possibilities.

"What if we have a trial period?" Astrid asked. "I'm not sure I wouldn't prefer to just cash in and move back to Norway, but I can admit that I also don't have much of a life there. I would like a challenge. I know Miranda said she doesn't want a job, but I do. I want some power. I want to be able to make decisions."

That would be one more thing to work out with Grant. Every bit of control to the wives took some away from him. "I think we can make that work. Three months to start and we regroup?"

Miranda looked out the window, pinching her lower lip between her thumb and index finger. "I can do that. But if any of us isn't happy after that time, we sell to Grant, agreed? If we hand over the reins to anyone, it should be him."

Tara wasn't necessarily vested in the idea of fostering loyalty to Grant, but Miranda was right. He was the obvious choice. After the three wives. "I'm fine with that."

"Me, too," Astrid said.

"We'll set up some sort of system where you report to me? So I can stay in the loop?" Miranda asked.

"Sure. I can send you an email or we can talk on the phone or whatever you want."

"Considering the legal ramifications, a letter on company letterhead might be best. Just to protect my own interests."

Okay, then. "Yes. Absolutely."

"And have you thought at all about what projects you want to pursue?"

"I'd like to see Sterling get in the mix with the Seaport Promenade project. It's a chance to work with the city and will be a very high-profile development."

A tiny grin crossed Miranda's face. "You know Johnathon was interested in pursuing that too but Grant squashed it. I'm not quite sure why."

"Interesting." Tara didn't want to start out by mowing down Grant's opinions of things, but she had a hunch she was right about the Seaport. "Speaking of which, Grant should be here in a bit to hear our answer to his proposal."

Miranda rose from her chair. "If it's all the same to you, I think I'll skip that part. I'm not good at delivering uncomfortable news. This was all your idea anyway."

"I'm not going to stay to tell him, either," Astrid said. "Thanks for the wine. Should I report to the office on Monday morning?"

Tara hadn't stopped to think out this level of logistics. "Let me talk to Grant first. I'll let you know when we need you."

Astrid's eyebrows popped up as she hitched her handbag over her shoulder. "When you need me? I own just as much of the company as you do. So I'd say you need me now."

Tara forced a smile. "Right. I'll figure something out as soon as possible."

Miranda and Astrid made their exit, leaving Tara feeling a bit like she was a lamb who'd been led to slaughter. Yes, this was her idea, but it was going to take all three wives to make it happen and it was clear that for now, this arrangement was tenuous at best. And then there was Grant to worry about. He would be pleased with none of this. It might be time to pour him a very stiff drink.

Grant pulled up in front of Tara's house, happy to have found street parking on the always busy Ocean Boulevard. He hopped out of his BMW, stuck with the realization that he was walking into the unknown. Tara, Miranda and Astrid could decide to go any number of directions. They could attempt to buy him out. Hell, they could try to unseat him as CEO. He wasn't ready to concede his dream. He'd spent too many years as the number-two person at Sterling, doing the dirty work and cleaning up after Johnathon's messes. Although one could argue that Grant was walking into yet another cleanup job.

He rang the doorbell and Tara quickly answered, wearing a white sweater that fell off her shoulder, revealing her silky-smooth skin, and a pair of jeans that showed off every inch of her lithe frame. He'd known the odds were stacked against him, but her outfit seemed a bit unfair. How was he supposed to concentrate when she looked so damn good? "Come on in," she said, waving him inside. "I have wine upstairs. Or bourbon if you prefer."

"Wine will be just fine." He followed her up the stairs, taking the chance to eye her hips in motion as she took each step. It was a glorious distraction from his worries about business. When they emerged on the top floor, to his great surprise, there was no sign of anyone else. "I thought Miranda and Astrid would still be here."

Tara was standing at the island in her spacious gourmet kitchen, pouring them each a glass of wine. "They left me as proxy." She clinked her glass with his. "Cheers."

He drew a long sip from his glass, her warm gaze connecting with his. She struck him as extremely relaxed right now, comfortable with whatever came next. Her steady demeanor was exactly the reason why she was so successful in real estate. Many of her clients found her presence incredibly calming. Of course, her adversaries thought she had nerves of steel. Grant found that it made his pulse race, but Tara had always had that effect on him. Even after all these years. Once again, he wondered about his loyalty to Johnathon and exactly how long he could stick to it. "So? Do you want to give me the answer? I'm guessing bad news since the other two decided to exit stage left."

"Come on." She took his hand and pulled him from the kitchen to the living room, then led him out to her sprawling balcony, wrapped around the front of the house with an unobstructed view of the beach and ocean beyond. Even with the picturesque setting and a beautiful woman holding on to his hand, Grant braced for the worst. She was being too calm. Too kind. "I don't want you to think of our answer as bad news. I think this could ultimately be a good thing for everyone."

That was all he truly needed to know. She was about to deliver an answer that was less than what he wanted. Still, he'd stick around for the explanation. And the wine. And the company, for that matter. When he wasn't focused on what Tara was about to do to his hopes and dreams, he couldn't deny his intense attraction, the way he wanted to wrap her up in his arms and kiss her. "Just say it, Tara. You're usually far more direct than this."

"Fine. The wives and I want to keep our shares. We want a role in running the company. On a temporary basis to start, and if all goes well, we want to make it permanent."

Grant rested his forearms on the railing, looking out over the vista. The sea breezes blew his hair back from his face. He should have seen this coming. Tara was incredibly driven. She saw opportunity and she took it. "I see."

She inched closer to him and put her hand on his back. For an instant, his eyes drifted shut and he soaked up her touch. He'd had countless thoughts over the years of moments like this, when he could be close to her. It had been his fantasy for so many years that it was nearly hardwired into his brain.

"That's it? You see?" she asked.

"I'm processing." He straightened, and as he'd feared, she let her hand drop. It was for the best, even if it disappointed him. The contact was driving him to distraction. It was too easy to think about his physical desires, when he needed to stay focused on business. "I don't think you three have any idea what you're signing up for. This business is brutal. Absolutely cutthroat."

"You think I don't know that? No, I don't do development now, but I work in a parallel universe. And I was there when you and Johnathon started the company. I know the nuts and bolts for sure. I also saw how hard he worked and how often he got cut down. Astrid and Miranda have witnessed the same. I think you're underestimating us. Plus, Miranda only wants a say in what happens with the company. She doesn't plan on taking an active role."

"Just you and Astrid, then? What is she qualified to do?"

"That, I don't know exactly. But I have to think we can find something for her."

"You know, this isn't a good time. Morale is very low. Everyone was crushed by Johnathon's death. This isn't a great time to bring in the Norwegian supermodel and let her take someone's job."

Tara shook her head. "We won't fire anyone, Grant. We just need to make room. I know there are parts of the company that are short staffed or have vacant positions."

"How exactly do you know that?"

"I have a friend who's an executive recruiter."

Grant took in a deep breath through his nose. There was an open job in project management that might work for Astrid, but that involved working closely with the architects on staff, and Miranda's brother Clay headed up that department. That seemed like a big potential problem. "What about Astrid and Miranda? Can you keep those two in check? They hate each other."

Tara took another sip of her wine. "Well, something sort of miraculous happened tonight. Astrid found out Miranda's pregnant and she didn't freak out. In fact, she congratulated her. I was pleasantly surprised."

"You have *got* to be kidding."

Tara shook her head. "I wouldn't kid about something like that."

So this was really happening. And he couldn't do anything to stop it. "What about you? Where do you fit into this equation?"

"I figured you and I could work together. You can show me the ropes. I can bring my real estate expertise and contacts into it. We could make a blockbuster team."

"Co-CEOs? I don't think so." That was not what he wanted. This was supposed to be his chance to step out of Johnathon's shadow and finally show the world how much he'd been responsible for making Sterling run all these years. It would be too easy to end up in a different Sterling shadow—Tara's.

"So call me an advisor to the CEO. I really don't care about titles."

It was so easy for Tara to set her ego aside. He admired that in her, among other things. "You realize we could have made a different kind of team at one point. Before you let Johnathon get in the way."

Tara knocked her head to the side and a lock of her hair fell across her beautiful face. She slowly swept it back. "I don't know, Grant. We have chemistry. We like to flirt. That's not the basis for a partnership. At least not the kind you're talking about."

"Every relationship starts with chemistry. Plus, you can't deny that you felt something the one time I kissed you."

"You promised we would never talk about that. I was engaged to Johnathon at the time."

Memories of that night flooded his mind. It was the one time he'd thought he might have a chance with her, although he hadn't taken the time to think out the repercussions. Johnathon never would've stood for it. It never could've been a long-term thing. "You'd broken up. You were about to call off the wedding."

Tara drew her lips into a tight and anxious bundle. "But I didn't call it off. I went through with it."

Grant didn't like to think about that day. It still hurt to think about his front-row seat to watching her say those vows to Johnathon. "Yes, you did."

"Look. It was an amazing kiss, but that doesn't mean the world. Plus, you wouldn't last five minutes with me. You're a nice guy. I don't do well with nice men. I tend to chew them up and spit them out and then I feel bad about it."

He'd heard that argument from other women and it made him nuts. He wasn't a nice guy. He merely refused to be a jerk. She could blame his wholesome midwestern upbringing, and a father who treated his mother like a queen. "You think you know me, but you don't."

"Well, it's not a good idea now anyway. We're about to be working together. It's never smart to mix business and pleasure."

If only Tara knew that as far as he was concerned, she was making a case for her to sell him her shares and let him take her to bed. But he didn't see tonight working out that way. "Only on a temporary basis?" He wasn't sure which part of their agreement he was talking about—the work side, or the romantic side, which was admittedly all in his head.

"We'll call it a trial."

"This conversation is a trial."

Tara laughed and it was such a boost to his sense of self, just at the right time, too. He was otherwise feeling a bit beat up. "Why? You're getting what you want. You're CEO of Sterling. And you're going to get to work with me every day, which you know will be fun."

Grant made a silent prayer for strength. He was about to walk into a less than optimal circum-stance—finally CEO of the company he'd been running from behind the scenes for years, while working side by side with the woman he'd never stopped wanting. He imagined he would be both incredibly excited to go to work every day and also filled with dread. "Promise? I could use a little fun."

"How about I promise to make it interesting?"

He wasn't happy that she hadn't taken the bait about having fun. He desperately needed that in his life. "I've had my fill of interesting. Let's focus on making it work."

"Don't worry about that. I absolutely will."

Five

The headquarters of Sterling Enterprises took up the top three floors of one of the newest, most exclusive high-rises in downtown San Diego. Johnathon had moved the company two years ago after overseeing the development of the building. Tara hadn't been to these new offices since the night of the grand opening reception, when Johnathon and Miranda were engaged to be married and Tara and Grant were engaged in a different way after a few glasses of champagne—burning through some high-octane flirtation.

Tara had actually considered kissing Grant that night. She'd had a full commentary running through her head as she weighed the pros and cons. *He's so hot. It should be criminal for a man to look that good in a suit. He laughs at my jokes. He notices when my drink needs refilling. And then there are those sweet, puppy-dog eyes of his.* She ultimately decided that it wasn't worth the risk. Johnathon would've gone ballistic, especially if he'd witnessed it, and Tara knew that she would only break Grant's heart. That was what she did, apparently, although not to men like Johnathon. Then it was he who did the breaking. Either way, Grant didn't deserve that. So she'd kept her hands and her lips to herself.

Now she was going to be working with that man who was all kinds of sexy, but all kinds of wrong for her. Luckily, she knew herself well enough to be certain that once she was in the work environment, any stray nonbusiness thoughts would evaporate. She was nothing less than laser focused when it came to any job. Grant would not distract her. She simply wouldn't let him.

Tara was rarely nervous, but she found herself feeling that way as she rode the elevator up to the offices. She'd never started a job near the top of the chain of command. She'd always worked her way from the bottom up. In real estate, it'd taken years to build her business and her reputation. One satisfied client brought many more. One big sale led to a bigger listing. Each day brought another rung on the ladder to reach for. At Sterling, she was about to start near the top, and that created a whole new level of pressure.

When the elevator doors slid open, she was taken

aback by the bustle of the office. It was noisy. And busy. The receptionist juggling the ringing phone, the arrival of visitors, parking validations and questions from employees breezing past her desk in a near-continuous stream back and forth. As Grant had promised, he was waiting for her, standing off to one side. He had his cell pressed to his ear. He caught sight of her and raised a finger to suggest he needed a moment. Tara stood and patiently waited until he finished his call. She tried to ignore how good he looked in his charcoal-gray suit. She needed to keep her eye on the prize—figuring out if working at Sterling Enterprises was going to be the key to her finally having the happiness she'd failed to find all these years.

"Reporting for work, Mr. Singleton," Tara quipped as soon as he'd hung up.

"You're late." Grant quirked one eyebrow at her, then waved her down the hall. "Come on. I'll show you your office."

Tara glanced at her phone. "It's five after nine. I couldn't find a parking space."

"Remind me and I'll get you an executive spot in the deck."

"That would be helpful. Thank you." Tara hustled up to walk alongside him. On paper, she might be his subordinate, but she still wanted him to see her as an equal. She and Grant could do great things together, but only as a team. "Is it always this busy first thing in the morning?"

"Yes. It's nonstop."

That was going to take some getting used to. Although she'd had her fair share of tense meetings and phone calls, Tara's office had normally been quiet and serene, by design. She liked calm. She got a lot done in an environment like that.

"Here you go," he said when they arrived at an office. "Will this work?"

Tara surveyed the space. It had a decent view of parts of downtown and the bay, but it was also too masculine. The walls needed a softer color. The furniture would need to be replaced. "I've only been here once, but isn't your office on the opposite end of this floor?"

"Yes."

"Next to Johnathon's, right?"

Grant cleared his throat and looked down at his shoes. "I'm in his office now."

"Oh, of course." It only made sense. He was CEO now. It was time for the company to move ahead. "So why not put me in your old space? We're going to be working together. Wouldn't that be easier?"

"I told you the other night. Morale is low right now. I didn't want too many big changes at one time."

Tara wasn't quite ready to challenge him on the idea of low morale, but the scene she'd walked into when she got off the elevator had seemed nothing short of lively. For now, she wouldn't make waves. "This will work. Long term, I'll want to make some changes."

"Maybe we should get through this three-month trial first." He stuffed his hands into his pockets. Everything in his body language said he was unhappy with her presence. He wandered over to the window and glanced outside, then turned back to her. "I've been meaning to ask, what have you done about your real estate clients?"

"I'm slowly phasing out. No new listings, no new buyers, and selling off what's already on the market. Then I'm done."

"That doesn't sound like a trial, Tara. That sounds permanent."

She set her laptop bag down on the desk and wound around to where he was standing. "The good thing about my business is that it's not hard to put it on pause. And I'd like for this to be permanent. I was not happy when Johnathon suggested I exit Sterling after the first few months. It didn't feel fair. I hardly got a chance."

"I know. He talked to me about it several times. Wondered if he was being a jerk about it."

"He said he didn't think it was good for our marriage, but I think he was threatened."

Grant looked at her, first scanning her face, but she couldn't help but notice the way he stole a gander at the rest of her, as well. From the glimmer in his eyes, he liked what he saw. "I can see that. You can be intimidating."

So much for thinking that look was one of admiration. Tara disliked being characterized that way.

She put herself in front of the world as a confident person because it got her the things she wanted. She never meant to be daunting. "I think he was worried that people would like me more than they liked him. He wanted everyone to worship him, even when he wasn't being nice."

"That's why he loved to make me the bad guy. He needed people to see him as the good one."

That had always been true of Johnathon. He often hid the unlikable parts of himself in an effort to get people to adore him. It was only the people closest to him who saw the real man. "Can I see what you did with Johnathon's office?"

Grant glanced at the Tag Heuer watch Johnathon had given him years ago. "I have a meeting in a few minutes. Why don't you get settled and we can chat later?"

She could see what he was doing and she disliked it greatly. "Grant. My getting settled is going to involve me opening my laptop and you telling me the WiFi password. Don't tuck me away in a corner and expect me to go away. I want to work. Let's talk about a project for me."

"Like?"

Tara already knew from Miranda that what she was about to say would be met with little enthusiasm. It didn't stop her from marching ahead. "The Seaport Promenade. It's a travesty that Sterling isn't in on this bidding process with the city and it isn't too late for us to make it happen."

As expected, Grant met her comment with a distinct scowl. "Not a good idea. It'll end up being nothing but a huge waste of time and resources."

"Well, gee. Tell me how you really feel."

"If you can't deal with my opinions on things, Tara, we're going to have some serious problems. I'm in charge now."

Tara had to wonder if perhaps this was Grant flexing his new muscle. She liked seeing him like this, showing some fight and exerting his control. She stepped closer and picked a fleck of lint from his jacket, then smoothed her hand over his lapel. "Of course you are. You're the boss and I'm here to learn."

Grant cleared his throat, staring down at her hand. "I know you're capable and smart, but there's still a lot you don't know about this side of real estate."

"Okay, then. I'm ready to learn. But if we're going to argue about Seaport Promenade, I think we should do it in your office." She made her way for the door, but cast a look back at him over her shoulder. "It's got to be more comfortable than mine."

One thing Tara had said was now permanently stuck in Grant's mind: *we should do it in your office.* He knew he shouldn't let his brain go there, but it had already happened, and now the rest of his body was having a field day with the idea. Grant felt as though all blood flow had left his brain for regions south. This was not a good start to his work day.

Against his better judgment, he gave in to her suggestion. "Come on. I'll postpone my meeting so we can talk this out."

He and Tara started down the hall to his office. Grant had no idea how he was going to live through this. Being around Tara was already an excruciating exercise in holding back and it had only been fifteen minutes. He'd spent the last decade not getting what he wanted. And now he couldn't have her, either. It would make everything too messy if they became involved, especially for the company.

Sterling was already on unsteady ground. He was truly torn about how best to handle Tara in the scope of the business—give her what she wanted in order to create less friction? Or fight her on it all and ultimately convince her that this trial of hers wasn't going to work? It was a conundrum for sure. He wanted to be with her. He'd wanted her for a decade. And this business idea of hers was ruining any chance of that.

They arrived at his office, on the exact opposite end of the building. He'd purposely put Tara as far away as possible. He hoped that she'd be less of a distraction. Perhaps things could ultimately play out that way, but for today, his strategy had failed. "Here you go." With a flourish of his hand, he welcomed her inside. "It still doesn't feel like mine. I have a feeling my job is going to be like that for a while, too." He didn't want to be vulnerable, but he knew he could be honest with Tara. If he wasn't, she'd probably figure it out anyway.

"But you've wanted this for a long time, right?"

Funny, but he'd always been sure that being in charge would make things better. Now that he was in this role he'd longed for, it wasn't yet feeling like everything he'd waited for. "What I've most wanted is the chance to run things the way I see fit. Johnathon and I butted heads a lot and he always managed to win. That got to be tiresome." It was no exaggeration. Johnathon came out on top with everything.

"So what are *you* wanting to tackle first?" Tara asked. "Anything in particular that you and Johnathon had been fighting over that wasn't going the way you wanted it to?"

"Well, since you put it that way, I have to tell you that my first priority was to put an end to any talk of pursuing the Seaport Promenade project. Johnathon really wanted to put in a bid with the city, but he wasn't the one who had to deal with the red tape."

The Seaport Promenade was a strip of property along the bay which was owned by the city. The current facilities included an aging park, some open space, and a small shopping center set to be knocked down. In its place would eventually be more ecologically friendly buildings, along with amenities to draw families to downtown. It was a big municipal contract, although there were certainly hoops to jump through. No city gave out a job like this without making sure they were getting everything they wanted.

"It's not my habit to agree with Johnathon, but I think it's a smart idea. I think we should go for it. It's such a high-profile project and it would be amazing publicity if we landed the contract."

"Your ex-husband pissed off a lot of people with the city. You have no idea the headache this would be."

"He was your best friend, too, you know. And he's not here to make people mad anymore. Let me try with the city. Let me see if we can throw our hat in the ring."

Grant pinched the bridge of his nose. A terrible headache was brewing. "It's not what we do. We do large private projects. Office buildings. Like this one. Big paydays. The margins are so thin with a government contract. I don't see the point."

Tara gestured to a chair opposite Grant's desk. "May I?"

"Be my guest."

She perched on the very edge of the seat and crossed her legs. He tried to ignore how amazingly sexy they were in her sky-high heels. "Look. You need to know how Sterling is seen in this town."

Grant stepped closer, unsure of where she was going with this. "I know our reputation. Smart. Nimble. Timely."

"You're also known as a bad neighbor. You only

go after massive projects, the big kill. Greed and profits at all costs is not a good look."

He could see some people viewing Sterling in that light. It still didn't make it easy to hear. "You keep saying *you*. You need to turn that into a *we*. We're in this together now. Working together, remember?"

"And you put me on the other end of the building. That's not togetherness. You're assuming I'm going to be a pain in your butt. It's fair."

If only Tara knew that the pain she was putting him through was of a different variety. It was probably time to go with his first idea—give in and take away the friction. "Okay. Fine. We can talk about Seaport Promenade. Why don't you call down to the city today and see where they are with the application process? I've been doing nothing but stalling this whole time, hoping Johnathon would get distracted by something else. For all I know, we've missed several key deadlines."

Just then, there was a knock on the door frame to Grant's office. It was Sandy, Johnathon's assistant. "Mr. Singleton, I'm sorry to bother you, but I don't know what I'm supposed to be doing today."

Grant sighed. He'd told Sandy to take last week off, but he'd forgotten to get back in touch with her about new responsibilities moving forward. Sandy was inexperienced, but she was an excellent employee—a self-starter who always arrived early and stayed late. "Yes, Sandy. I'm sorry. Come on in." Grant gestured for her to have a seat. "I want you to meet Tara Sterling. I'll be working with her over the next several months, keeping our heads above water as we move forward without Mr. Sterling."

Sandy offered her hand to shake Tara's. "I know who you are, Ms. Sterling. I've seen your Realtor ads on the bus benches."

Tara smiled warmly. "Well, I'm moving out of selling and into developing. Hopefully you won't have to look at those ads too much longer."

"I'd love to hear more about what you used to do. I'm interested in all aspects of real estate." Sandy took a seat next to Tara.

All of this was giving Grant an idea. He needed a place to put Sandy and he needed a way to keep Tara preoccupied for at least part of the day. He had work to do and a lot of it. "Sandy, I apologize for springing this on you at the spur of the moment, but how would you feel about working for Ms. Sterling? As her admin? It seems like a logical step. You know the ins and outs of the various projects we're working on right now. And you know everyone in the office and how things run."

"I'd be happy to work for Ms. Sterling. I'd love it, in fact."

That was one less organizational challenge Grant needed to face today. He was thankful for that. "Perfect."

Tara nodded, but seemed wary of having this new person foisted upon her. "Sandy, maybe you and I can brainstorm some changes to my office when you have a minute. If I'm going to be over in no-man's land, I might as well make it look good."

"Sure thing, Ms. Sterling. Whatever you need."

Tara rose from her chair. "Okay, then." She made her way for the door, following Sandy, but she stopped at Grant's side. "On my way to the other end of the building now. I'll call you when I get there. Should probably only take an hour." She cocked an eyebrow at him.

"Tara. It wasn't personal. I made a choice, okay?" Except that it *was* personal. Everything between them would always be that way.

"It feels a bit intentional. I'm not hurt. Just don't want to let you off the hook too easy."

If only she knew that deep down, he wanted to be on her hook. He might already be on it. "Would it make you happier if you had my old office?"

"It would. It would certainly send a better message to the rest of the company regarding my role."

Grant drew in a deep breath through his nose. "Okay. But let's get maintenance in there to paint first. The walls are scuffed up. It should be nice."

"You get a little wild and crazy a few times in there, Grant?"

"More like tired and frustrated. I might have kicked the wall once or twice, but only out of exasperation."

A crease formed between her eyes as she narrowed her sights on him. "I keep giving you opportunities to flirt with me and you aren't taking the bait. Are you feeling okay?"

I need you to give up this crazy idea of yours. "That's for after work. You know that." He regretted the words the instant they left his mouth. He should have said that he and Tara were done flirting, forever.

"Okay. What are you doing tomorrow night?"

Grant blinked so fast it nearly knocked one of his contact lenses out of his eye. "What?"

"I have an invite to a party hosted by a friend of mine. Another real estate agent. It's on the rooftop of the Sussex Building. It has an amazing view of the ballpark and there's a game going on during the party."

"Why not take Miranda? Or Astrid? They're your closest confidantes these days, aren't they?"

"But they're not as much fun as you are."

Grant found it difficult to swallow. His mouth had gone incredibly dry.

"Just say yes," she continued. "It'll be good for you. Get out. See some people. Maybe squeeze in some flirting?"

He hated the way the heat rose in his cheeks. It was so damn predictable. "I like baseball."

Tara elbowed him in the ribs. "Oh, come on. You like me, too. I know you do."

Six

The Sussex building was only a few blocks from Sterling Enterprises, so Tara and Grant walked over after work. The day had been unremarkable—Grant was always in meetings, which left Tara stumbling around in the dark trying to sort out the process for the Seaport Promenade pitch. Sandy had been an invaluable resource, dealing with the city directly and gathering the needed information.

"How are you feeling about Seaport after your first two days?" Grant asked.

"Good, so far. We need to meet with Clay as soon as Sandy and I are done pulling the basics together. We have six weeks before we need to present. Do you think that's doable?"

Grant opened the door when they reached the address for the party. "It'll be tight, but I think we can make it work."

They presented their security passes and Tara pressed the button for the fifteenth floor. "Hold on a minute. You almost sound enthusiastic for this idea."

They stepped onto the elevator and rode up alone. "I don't have to do the hard work. That's all on you."

"Would you consider being there for the presentation to the city? It might help with our credibility."

Grant looked at the numbers light up as they reached each new floor. "I'll think about it."

Tara decided not to push it, but this seemed like yet another example of Grant creating distance between them. It didn't bode well for her future at Sterling, being an integral part of the team. She was going to have to keep pushing.

They reached the top floor of the building and stepped out into the lavish party space. Tara had been to several wedding receptions and extravagant bashes there, and it was a jaw-dropping location for festivities. Inside the expansive lounge area, partygoers chattered away on chic black leather sofas, enjoyed drinks at high-top tables and nabbed passed appetizers from the waitstaff, all against the backdrop of a stunning city view provided by floor-to-ceiling windows. But the real showstopper was the outdoor area just off the main room, with a glitzy fireplace taking the edge off the nighttime chill in the air, and bar tables for two alongside the balcony's unique glass railing.

The panorama was spectacular—a view of the baseball stadium below, the green field all lit up and the muffled sounds of the game floating up to their high perch. They were surrounded by shorter buildings, and off in the distance, you could see the dark ripples of the bay and the soaring steel structure of the bridge to Coronado.

Tara loved this city, just as Johnathon had, and she hoped that her role at Sterling could prove that point. She was eager to do more than drag Grant begrudgingly along with the idea of pursuing the Seaport Promenade project. She wanted to prove to him that it was worthwhile. It wasn't folly. She had the vision. It might not bring the money rolling in right away, but it was important to be a part of the community and make a contribution that would pay off in the long term.

The party was casual, but still a business affair, and Grant had dressed accordingly, in charcoal trousers and a pale blue dress shirt that really brought out his eyes. It wasn't conjecture to say her date was the best-looking guy at the party. It was a fact. Of course, flirtation aside, this was no date. It was a chance for two colleagues and friends to spend some time together. She wanted Grant and her to be close again. It could only help when it came to work.

After they made small talk with several agents Tara knew, Grant seemed antsy. "Can I get you something to drink?" he asked, gently placing his hand at the small of her back.

It was nice to have the male attention, to have someone take care of her for once. She was usually so busy being independent. "Sure. I'll take a beer. An IPA if they have it."

"It's San Diego. I'm sure they'll have one."

Grant wandered off, and Tara finished up her conversation, realizing just how glad she was to be making a shift in her career. All this talk of house showings and demanding clients was tiresome. She was happy she didn't have to wake up tomorrow morning to that reality. When Grant returned with their beers, Tara wanted the chance to move on to something different. "You'll have to excuse us. Grant and I want to check out the game."

They stepped out onto the balcony and into the slightly cooler night air. "It's an amazing way to see a baseball game, huh?" Tara asked.

Grant shook his head and leaned against the railing. Tara was not so brave. She loved the view, but hated heights, so she stood back from the edge. "We are not at a baseball game. We're at a business function with a sport being played nearby. The players are like ants. You can't follow the ball."

Tara was a bit disappointed. She'd hoped Grant would enjoy this outing and he clearly was not having fun. She'd wanted this to be a time for them to bond. "There's free beer though. Hard to complain about that."

"I'm not complaining. I just find it funny that this group of people thinks we're at a baseball game.

This is for someone who doesn't care about the sport, which is fine. But call it what it is."

"A schmoozefest?"

He straightened and pointed his beer bottle at her, a slight smile breaking across his face. "Exactly."

Tara again surveyed the crowd of beautiful people, talking away about their jobs and their successes. No one mentioned their failures at an event like this, or even their struggles. It was all to put on a good face. Tara could see why Grant found it annoyingly empty.

"I recognize the value in seeing and being seen," Grant continued. "But it always feels so phony to me. Johnathon was better at this than I am. I don't enjoy playing the game. I'd much prefer to simply do the work."

"Is that why you don't want to pursue Seaport?" she asked. "Too many politics to play?"

"In part, yes. And the person who played the politics before us left behind a steep uphill climb."

Grant had given Tara even more to think about, but then she got distracted by a glimpse of a man over at the bar. She didn't want to stare, but she couldn't help it. Needing confirmation, she grabbed Grant's arm and popped up onto her tiptoes, whispering into his ear. "Am I crazy or is that Johnathon's brother Andrew over there?" Not wanting to be too obvious, she grasped his other hand so she was facing him. "Right over my shoulder. Ordering a drink."

Grant scoped out the scene, then dropped his

sights to Tara. His eyes were intense. Nearly blazing. "What in the hell is he doing in San Diego? He couldn't come to his own brother's funeral two weeks ago, but he could come down here for a party or a baseball game?" Grant rarely had a reaction that heated. Tara couldn't ignore how much more attracted she was to him when he was being this way.

"This is not a baseball game. You were very clear about that."

Grant finished his beer and clunked the bottle down on a nearby table. "This is weird, Tara. And I don't like it."

"Yeah. Me neither." Tara rolled her head to one side and glanced back at Andrew. He looked so much like Johnathon, it was uncanny. Same handsome features, same head of thick brown hair. Tara hadn't laid eyes on Andrew since her own wedding, back when he and Johnathon were still on speaking terms. Soon after, Sterling Enterprises was launched. Johnathon offered Andrew a job, but that inexplicably created a deep rift between the brothers. Johnathon was only trying to help after Andrew's first attempt at his own development firm had failed. The brothers stopped speaking to each other, and Andrew moved to Seattle because of it, starting a second company in a market where he wouldn't have to compete against Johnathon. "Should we go talk to him?"

"And say what? Tell him he's a jerk for not attending his own brother's funeral? I want nothing to do with that guy. At all." Grant turned his head, tracking Andrew across the room.

Tara looked back again. Andrew was winding his way through the crowd, away from them. "Is he leaving?"

"I hope so."

Tara didn't want to let this opportunity go. It wasn't right that Andrew hadn't been at Johnathon's funeral. And she knew Grant felt that way, too. "Come on. We can't let this go. We need to talk to him." She grabbed Grant's hand and led him across the room, weaving past the other guests, some of whom were trying to stop her to talk.

"Every time you lead me somewhere, something bad happens. Case in point, the other night out on your balcony."

"Shush. This has to be done." With one last tug on Grant's hand, they emerged from the crowd and out into the elevator vestibule. Andrew was standing there, checking his phone. "Andrew," she said, clearly.

He looked up, shock coloring his face. "Tara. Grant. This is a surprise."

Before Tara had a chance to respond, Grant dropped her hand and confronted Andrew. "That's bull and you know it. You had to have seen us inside. Is that why you're leaving?"

Andrew fumbled with his phone and slid it into his back pocket. He seemed nothing short of nervous. Good. Let him be put on the spot. "I didn't see you. And I was only here for a moment. I had a friend who was here, but this isn't really my scene."

"You didn't come to the funeral." Grant took a solid step forward, nearly encroaching on Andrew's personal space. "You told me you would try to make it."

Andrew jabbed the elevator button several times, as if that would make it appear faster. "I was busy. Something came up."

"Okay," Grant said, sounding nothing short of skeptical. "Why come to town now?"

"Business."

"Anything I need to know about? This isn't exactly your corner of the world."

Andrew slid Grant an unkind look. "Just a partnership. I didn't come to town to step on your toes if that's what you think."

"And yet you still couldn't make the funeral."

"Look, it's not like Johnathon would've known I was there. Funerals are for the living and nobody at that funeral cares whether or not I show up."

"I cared. I cared a lot. You weren't there for your brother. It's not right." Grant's voice was resolute. For someone who wanted nothing to do with Andrew, he was having no problem speaking his mind to him.

"It wasn't nice, Andrew," Tara said. "Johnathon was always there for you."

Andrew shook his head. "Not always." The elevator door slid open and he quickly stepped inside.

Grant lunged to hold it open. "Johnathon's wife, Miranda, is pregnant. You're going to be an uncle."

It was Andrew's turn to step in the way of the door and keep it from closing. "Wait. What?"

"It's true," Tara said, wanting to take part in this, although she wasn't entirely sure why Grant would choose to divulge this piece of information. It was still early in Miranda's pregnancy. Did she want everyone to know about it?

Andrew blew out a deep breath. "Well, give her my best."

"Or you could call and tell her yourself, then apologize for missing Johnathon's service," Grant said.

"I'm heading to the airport right now and flying home to Seattle. I'll call her soon."

"Just don't be a jerk, okay? She's been through a lot." Grant stepped back.

Andrew did the same. The elevator doors whooshed shut. And he was gone.

"Wow. That was weird," Tara said.

"It was infuriating—that's what that was." Grant wandered over to a small window and pounded the side of his fist against the frame. She loved seeing this side of him—fiery and passionate. She wished he'd be like this more often. "You know, I had plenty of problems with Johnathon, but he was nothing short of an amazing person. Andrew was his only family on this earth, and he couldn't show up when it mattered? It's pathetic." He turned back to Tara and she could see the fire in his eyes again. She understood what a confluence of emotions Johnathon brought up, and she admired that Grant wasn't afraid to show it. He was being brave in ways she wasn't always able to be.

"I'm sorry that happened. It was my idea to talk to him. I should've just let him leave."

Grant shook his head and reached out for Tara's arm, dragging his fingers down the back of it until he reached her hand. "No. It was a good thing." His voice was quieter now. "I needed to say those things to him and Andrew needed to hear them, even if he didn't know it. You push me, Tara, and that's a good thing."

His statement brought a smile to her face, but it also sent goose bumps racing over the surface of her skin. The idea of her and Grant as a team wasn't hopeless. She knew they could work together well. She just needed to prove it to him. "Does that mean I can push you on the Seaport Promenade?"

A breathy laugh escaped his lips and he raked his hands through his hair. At that moment, Tara fought an intense urge to kiss him, or at the very least, take the chance to run her own fingers into the dark mop atop his head. "It might take a lot of pushing."

"I'm up to the task."

Grant pressed the button to call the elevator back to their floor. "Let's get out of here. I don't need any more free beer or fake conversation."

"What did you have in mind?" Tara was thinking that a drive to her place might be in order. They could open a bottle of wine. She could try to press him some more on the Seaport project.

"Let's walk over to the ballpark, buy some tickets and watch the rest of the game. From actual seats. Not a luxury box."

"It's got to be the fourth inning, at least."

"So? Still plenty of baseball to be played."

"Neither of us is dressed for it." She looked down at her clothes. She was wearing heels, a black skirt and a silver silk blouse. Not exactly the right attire for a sporting event.

The elevator dinged. "Something tells me they'll still take our money."

With a beer in his hand and Tara at his side, Grant was having the most fun he'd had in…well, he couldn't remember a time he'd had more fun. "This was one of my best ideas, ever."

Tara popped some popcorn into her mouth, then licked the salt from her fingers. "We can definitely see a lot better. I'm just not sure it was worth it to drop five hundred bucks on seats right behind home plate when we aren't even going to see the whole game."

Grant reached over and took a handful of popcorn. "You only live once. I'd say it was worth every penny."

She cast a smile at him, which made his entire body warmer. "The view is so much better close up."

You're so much better close up.

He sat back and draped his arm across the back of Tara's seat. He didn't buy this whole notion that he was a nice guy and therefore not right for her. In fact, he thought it was complete bull. He'd proved back at the Sussex that he was capable of being a jerk when needed, and more important, he could tell that she appreciated having nice things done for her.

No, as far as Grant was concerned, the big thing standing between Tara and him was Sterling Enterprises. It was one thing for the founder's ex-wife to show up on staff because she'd inherited a chunk of the company. It was quite another for her to take up with the new CEO. There would be talk, and that would prompt questions about Grant's fitness for his role. He'd worked too hard to let a romance with Tara get in his way.

Still, he was all kinds of tempted. He couldn't take his eyes off her, even when she was distracted by the game and everything going on around them. He was only vaguely aware of the rest of the world. Her beauty demanded his focus, but it was about more than her flawless facade. He knew what was behind the pretty face and kissable lips. Tara was smart as a whip and a total handful. Full of life and surprises.

A chant of voices broke out around them, growing louder and louder. *What are they saying?* One word, over and over again. *Kiss?* Tara looked up. She pointed at the mammoth television monitor nearest them and laughed. Grant followed her line of sight and there they were onscreen, just the two of them. They looked amazing together. Absolutely perfect.

Before he knew what was happening, Tara's mouth was zeroing in on his. "We have to kiss."

"What?"

"We're on the kiss cam." She placed her hand on his cheek and angled his face toward hers.

Finally, Grant's brain clicked in on what was happening and he went for it with all of the enthusiasm of a kid who has just discovered an unguarded cookie jar. His hand shot to her jaw, then his fingertips were curling into the soft skin of her neck. With his other arm he pulled her closer. Their lips met. She was everything he'd remembered from the last time they did this. Ripples of electricity ran through his body as she parted her lips and gently nudged his lower lip with her tongue.

And then it was over. She pulled away from him, but they remained entangled. His arm was still holding her close. His chest heaved as he tried to breathe in her scent as much as humanly possible.

"That was fun," she said, the color rising in her cheeks.

"It was more than that, Tara." *I want you.* He wasn't sure he'd ever wanted anything or anyone as much as he wanted her at that moment. It was more than sexual desire, although that had been so firmly planted in his brain he wasn't sure he'd ever forget it. This was about quenching a thirst. One that had gone unsatisfied since the moment he met her.

She smiled and granted him another peck, this one on the cheek. "You're too handsome for your own good. You know that, right?"

"Thanks. Do you want to get out of here?" The words rushed from his mouth before he had a chance to think about them. That was definitely for the best. There was something magical about this moment and he wasn't about to let it slip between his fingers.

"You don't want to stay for the rest of the game?"

"I don't."

She cast him some side-eye. "Can I show you something first?"

He gathered their drink cups and stood. "Absolutely."

With no time to waste, they scooted past the other fans in their aisle, then up the concrete stadium stairs and out onto the concourse. He took her hand, but he let her lead the way out to the sidewalk. "This way." With the streets closed off to traffic, she didn't need to look for cars as she led him across the boulevard and to the other side.

"Where are we going?"

"The promenade site. I want to show you my idea."

Grant didn't want to encourage Tara. Except that he did. Her enthusiasm was infectious. It was like an electrical jolt to the system and he quite frankly couldn't get enough. "Yeah. Sure. Let's go."

They wound their way between buildings and emerged out by the bay, with the wide promenade extending in either direction along the water. The night air was cooler here, the breeze strong, blowing Tara's hair every which way.

"Picture this," she said, swiping her hands in midair as if she was washing windows. "An open-air food hall, with tons of outdoor seating and space beyond for food trucks. We put in artificial turf for kids to play." She turned to Grant as she forged ahead down the sidewalk. "Soft, of course. We don't want anyone getting hurt, but it is more eco-friendly. Beyond that, we put in a shopping pavilion with more outdoor space for seasonal markets. The city could invite farmers in during spring and summer, and there could be one at Christmas, as well. Or the Fourth of July. We could add a large stage area for performances of all kinds. Music and dance. It would be a real destination. Families, retirees, young people."

"And no high-rises? There's density to consider in downtown. The city is going to want to know that you're giving them the most bang for their buck."

"We're already surrounded by big buildings. I think that with the right architect, you'd have no problem maximizing the square footage. And you put in lots of multipurpose space. You'd have to be smart and innovative about it." She looked off in the distance at what was there right now, the outdated facilities the city was set to soon demolish, and it was as if she could see it all.

"I had no idea you had such a vision for this."

"Does that make you more inclined to want to pursue it? Because I have more ideas. Lots more."

He was tempted to tell her that he might agree to anything she wanted right now. "Wow. Seriously?"

She turned to him, her face lit up with excitement. It was intoxicating and infectious. She was a wonder. "I get it from my dad. He was a contractor, but he'd always wanted to be an architect. He could see things other people couldn't."

This was the first time Tara had ever talked about her family in front of him. Everything Grant knew was secondhand information he'd gotten from Johnathon. "Your mom passed away when you were young, didn't she?"

Tara pressed her lips together firmly, seeming caught off guard. "Johnathon told you that."

"He did. Is it difficult for you to talk about?"

She turned away from him. "It's not my favorite topic if that's what you're asking."

"I'm sorry. I'm just trying to peel back the layers a little bit here. That's all. Your dad clearly meant a lot to you."

Again she turned, this time to face him. The wind had picked up and Tara was leaning right into it. It was like everything she did—facing it all head-on. "He meant everything. He was my rock my entire life. He was the one man in my life who never let me down."

It broke his heart to hear that. He made a silent

vow to never be a man who would let her down. "Obviously you don't put Johnathon in that category."

"I loved him, but I didn't love the fact that he basically got bored with me. No one wants to feel like that. I wasn't the shiny new toy anymore. I wasn't Astrid, that's for sure."

He hated hearing Tara talk about herself like that, but she wasn't off base. Johnathon had been pure of heart, but he'd also let the wind carry him in many directions. He always found a way to rationalize his changing allegiances. *Tara's better off without me*, he'd said to Grant when he'd decided it was over with her. All Grant could think at the time was that Johnathon was a damn fool—a fool who covered all his bases, since he was quick to add one warning to his best friend. *I'm begging you. Please don't go there. I've seen the way you look at her. It would kill me if you and Tara ever became a thing.*

And so Grant had abided by Johnathon's wishes. But things were different now. And he was tired of wasting precious time. "I told him he was an idiot when he left you."

"No you did not."

Grant nodded. "I did. Not that it was in my best interest."

"He hated being criticized."

"It had to be said." Did Grant have the nerve to tell Tara the way he'd really felt that day? The way he'd felt before then, when it had been sheer torture to see his best friend married to the woman he'd always wanted? It seemed too heavy a topic for a moment like this, especially now that they were working together. "I told him that only someone stupid would walk away from you. I never would've done that. Not if I'd been the one who was with you."

She smiled and nodded. "You're a loyal guy. Everyone knows that about you."

She wasn't getting the point. This wasn't about him. It was about her. He stepped closer and put his hand at her elbow. "Loyal to a point."

"I don't know if that's true. You can be pushed pretty far."

"Everyone has their breaking point. I think mine actually happened tonight. When we kissed." Their gazes connected and he welcomed the jolt of electricity between them. It didn't seem possible she didn't feel it, too.

She leaned into him and put her hand on his shoulder. "That was nice."

"It was better than nice, Tara. It was amazing." He threaded his fingers through her hair, cupped her jaw and brought her mouth to his. Now that they were away from the crowd and the cameras, the importance of the kiss was magnified. He wanted Tara. He'd wanted her for too long. And this might be his only chance with her.

Which meant that for tonight, he was going to turn his back on his promise to Johnathon. He dared to break free from the kiss. Tara looked up at him, mouth slack and beckoning. If he wasn't afraid of violating a few public-decency laws, he would've made love to her right then and there. But he wanted a bed. And privacy. And time. "I think we need to get out of here. Together. Now."

It felt like a lifetime until she replied. "Let's go get your car."

Seven

Tara had never traveled over the bridge so quickly. Grant zipped through traffic like a man on a mission. For a moment she found herself wondering why. Yes, their attraction had been simmering away for years. Was that it? Too much buildup? Or was there something more?

He parked his BMW out in front of her house and they both did their best to not act as though they were rushing as they hurried to her gate, then through the courtyard beyond, leading to the front door. There was a part of this that made her feel like a teenager—making a choice she knew wasn't smart. Granted, she'd done exactly everything she was supposed to do when she was younger. She never disappointed her dad. Ever.

Tara keyed her way in through the door, but Grant didn't wait, taking her handbag and plopping it on the entry table, then threading both hands against her neck and combing his fingers into her hair. He raised her lips to his and claimed them, his mouth open and wet. Commanding. Taking everything he wanted. Tara gave it all enthusiastically. She'd always suspected Grant would be passionate, but not like this. Not so eager to be in charge.

"Do you want to go upstairs?" she asked breathlessly.

"Not yet." He pinned her against the wall with his body weight and reached for the hem of her skirt. He hitched one side up over her hip. "I want you to come for me, first."

Whatever you want raced through her head, but then she got lightheaded from the intensity of his kiss.

His fingers sped through the buttons of her blouse and he pulled it back, revealing her lacy bra. Grant's eyes were dark in the soft light of the foyer, and Tara felt like she was seeing a different side of him. So sexy. So red-blooded. He pulled down the cup of her bra with no hesitation. The combination of cool air against her skin, and the realization that he was going to touch her there made her nipple tighten, a rush of blood making her breast heavy. She nearly bucked against him. He pinched her already taut skin, scanning her face for a reaction. Raising her chin, she met his gaze, not to be outdone by him, but her mouth dropped open. It felt too good as he plucked at the hard bud. It sent sizzles of electricity down the length of her torso, aimed right between her legs.

He gathered her hands and raised them above her head, pinning them against the wall with one hand while the other slipped down the front of her panties. He pressed against her hard with his torso as his fingers found her center. Her most delicate and sensitive spot. The place where she most yearned for his touch. He nuzzled his face into her neck and kissed and licked, all while keeping her pinned in place and working her apex in tight circles with his nimble fingers. There was zero question in her mind as to whether Grant knew what he was doing. He was playing her like a fiddle, and she was completely at his mercy.

Tara's eyes drifted open and shut, then open and shut again as the pleasure wound through her. There was too much thrill of the new, too much excitement from the unexpected. This was wrong. So wrong. And that made it feel so right.

"You are so damn sexy," Grant growled into her ear. He bit her neck softly; he licked her skin. His mouth was sheer heaven and part of her really hoped that she'd get to experience it all over her body tonight.

"So are you," she muttered, her thoughts so disjointed it was like her head was in the clouds. "I had no idea you'd be like this."

"Like what? Not nice?"

He moved to the other side of her neck, but he slid his fingers down lower and slipped one inside her. He thrust hard, the heel of his hand hitting her apex, over and over again. *Damn.* She was so close to the peak she could hardly think straight. "Everything you're doing right now is better than nice." *So much better.*

Tara's breaths were so ragged it was as if they were being ripped from her lungs. All the while the pressure was building between her legs and her knees were growing weaker. Grant squeezed her wrists hard, pressing them into the wall as she thrust her hips forward, needing more. Craving. Wanting. Finally the orgasm tore through her and she called out, a cry that was quickly extinguished by the crush of Grant's mouth. He kissed her deeply and with a passion she'd never experienced. It was raw and untamed, nothing but pure want. Their tongues wound together in a languid circle as he slowed the passes with his finger, but didn't relinquish control. She didn't begrudge him any of it. It was the sexiest thing she'd experienced in, well, quite frankly, ever.

She buried her face in his neck as she rode out the final waves of pleasure. She kissed his Adam's apple, which seemed to be bulging from his neck. "I want to make you happy," she said, realizing too late that it might sound like more of a promise than she was willing to keep.

"Good. Because that's just the start."

He let go of her hands and Tara collected herself,

tugging down her skirt, but not bothering with buttoning her blouse. It wasn't going to be on long. She kicked off her heels as Grant removed his suit coat, then she took his hand and led him upstairs.

As soon as they were in her room, she began working on his shirt, eager to get rid of it and start exploring his body the way he had hers. The sight of his chest and bare shoulders elicited a groan from deep in her throat. He was broad and firm with a lovely patch of dark hair in the center. He'd been working out and she was going to reap the benefits. She kissed his pecs, her fingers curling into his defined and muscular biceps. He threaded his hands inside her blouse and pushed it from her shoulders, then teased her by tracing his fingers up and down the channel of her back, over the strap of her bra, bypassing the chance to take it off. Tara shifted one hand from his arm to the front of his pants, where his steely erection was waiting for her. She pressed against his length and he groaned his approval. She rubbed up and down, using a delicate pressure, just enough to make him harder.

"What do you want, Grant?"

He reached for her chin and raised it so that they were gazing into each other's eyes. "I want everything you want to give me. Absolutely everything."

It was like she was breathing in his words and they served only to embolden her. She wanted to rock his world. She wanted tonight to be memorable. This had to be a one-time thing. There was too much on the line with their shared business interests for it to be anything more than that. That was the only coherent thought she could muster.

She kissed him one more time to make sure this was what she wanted. The way he pulled her into his arms and dug his fingers into the back of her hair spoke of possessiveness. He was being dominant and she loved every minute of it. This was not a characteristic she expected from Grant, the good-looking guy next door. The heartbreaker with the puppy-dog eyes. And so she went with it, just to see what was next.

Grant was so overwhelmed by the sensory pleasure of having Tara half-naked in his arms that all logical thought was gone. His body and mind had been at war, and his brain had been defeated. This was Tara. The woman he'd wanted for so long. The woman he'd fantasized about hundreds of times. Her beautiful body was at his command right now. She was his for the taking. And there was part of him that was telling his brain to keep track of every unbelievable detail. The curve of her hips under his hand, the creamy skin of her breasts and the sweet sin of her mouth.

He kissed her deeply and then led her over to the bed, where he perched on the very edge. "I want to watch you undress."

A coy smile crossed her lips, which made his erection that much harder. He ached for her so badly it was hard to believe he'd ever be able to walk again. "You naughty boy," she said, pushing on his chest with a playful nudge.

Grant eased back on his elbows, wishing his pants were off. He could hardly stand the strain of his rigid length against his boxer briefs. Still, he relished the view as Tara, still wearing her black lace bra, unzipped her skirt with her back to him. She looked over her shoulder, her bright eyes conveying everything he'd ever wanted in a single glance. She wriggled it past her hips, bending at the waist and giving him a magnificent view of her backside in matching panties. She stepped out of the skirt and reached back to unhook her bra, nudging it from each shoulder as if she was a burlesque dancer accustomed to giving the audience the best possible show. He was dying of anticipation, but it was so worth the wait when she dropped the garment to the floor and turned around to face him. Her breasts were simply magnificent and he couldn't wait to have them in his hands again. To take her nipples between his lips.

She stepped closer and dropped to her knees before him. His heart was about to pound its way through his chest as he watched her delicate fingers unclasp his belt and unzip his trousers. He raised his hips from the bed as she tugged them down, taking his boxer briefs at the same time. That first brush of her fingertips against his length was like a rocket straight to the center of his body. It made him lightheaded. It made him delirious and thankful and hundreds of other things he couldn't begin to put a label on. He did his best to stay grounded in the moment as she took him in her hand and stroked firmly.

If only she knew that every single thing she did only made him want and need her even more. As she rolled her thumb over the tip when she reached the top, he thought he might pass out. If he didn't concentrate and get with the program, he was going to come from only a few passes. He focused on her, on the beauty of her face and on the recollection that he'd waited too long for this to be anything less than perfect.

Still, when she lowered her head and took him into her mouth, his mind and body resumed their battle, and this time, it was a full-body campaign. He could hardly believe this was happening. He eased his head back on the bed and combed his fingers into her hair, trying to wrap his mind around her hot and velvety lips riding his length. Luckily, she knew to take things slowly and carefully. She didn't apply too much pressure, just enough to make him wish that this moment would go on forever. When she loosened the grip of her lips, he was disappointed for only a second. He opened his eyes to watch her removing her panties, then she straddled him on the bed, bracketing his hips with her knees.

She ground her center against his erection, which was an awful lot of physical gratification considering how badly he wanted to be inside her. She was wet and warm against his length and she was clearly enjoying it, as she moaned softly and dropped her head to one shoulder, her beautiful blond hair cascading to the side. It was a vision worth holding on to, but he needed to make love to her the way he needed air and water.

"Do you have a condom?" he asked.

She hopped off the bed so quickly it was as if she had anticipated the question. "I do." Sliding the bedside-table drawer open, she pulled out a foil packet, tore it open and rolled it onto his length. She then stretched out next to him on the bed. He rolled to his side and kissed her, cupping her breast with his hand, relishing the velvety feel of her skin against his. Tara rolled to her back and he followed, positioning himself between her legs. She let her knees drop to the bed and he took another moment to admire her beauty before he drove inside. Her body welcomed him, then gathered around him tightly, wrapping him up in the most mind-blowing heat. He was overwhelmed by the sensations as they began to move together. She was perfect. Exactly as he'd always hoped.

He focused on her breaths as he found the perfect spot to deliver the pressure he knew she'd need. The tension coiled deep in his belly, pulling tighter and tighter until he was worried he couldn't take it much longer. But Tara was showing her own signs of approaching that blissful moment when you come undone and still want more. She dug her heels into the backs of his thighs, meeting his every thrust with a forceful rock of her hips. A few more thrusts and she fell apart, tossing her head back on the bed and thrashing from side to side. Grant sucked in a deep breath as he felt the dam break and wave after wave of intense pleasure rolled through him. He closed his eyes and let every serious thought of friendship and foes, and love and loyalty float away. He knew that they would return, but for now, everything was perfect.

Eight

Tara didn't like the idea of regret over sleeping with Grant. But in the light of day, as the early-morning sun streamed in through her bedroom window, casting him in a golden glow, she was torn. Last night had been incredible, and it had been too long since she'd had a man in her bed. But her choice of man might not have been the best. She hadn't been looking at the long-term ramifications last night. She'd only been looking at how hot Grant was, and reacting to the pure power of his kiss.

But she couldn't afford for her position with Sterling to be compromised, not when she was just getting started. A woman couldn't start work at the company her dead ex-husband had founded, sleep with the CEO and expect her colleagues to hold her in high esteem. It simply wasn't how things worked in the real world.

"Last night was amazing." She didn't want to lay it on too thick, but Grant had earned the accolade. Tara smoothed her hand over his sculpted shoulder and kissed his collarbone, allowing her lips to linger a few extra heartbeats. Now that they'd had sex, it was impossible to be around him and not touch him. She was going to have to find a remedy to that.

"What time is it?" He had one eye open and the other closed. His voice was groggy and sleepy. So sexy.

"A little before seven. I wasn't sure what time you wanted to get up. You must want to get back to your place to get dressed for work."

Grant groaned and rolled to his side, draping his arm across her waist and then pulling her closer. "Let's call in sick. No one will care if we aren't there."

"You're the boss. Everyone will care."

He drew in a deep breath and blew it out, seeming duly exasperated. "I suppose you're right. Still doesn't make it any better."

Tara was about to agree with him when the doorbell rang. For a moment, she and Grant looked at each other in confusion, and then it dawned on her. "It's probably Britney next door. She's always complaining that my sprinklers are watering the sidewalk. Her dog doesn't like it. He has very sensitive paws." She threw back the covers and grabbed her silk robe from the chair opposite the bed. She loved seeing her clothes and Grant's mingling on the floor, a distinct trail leading from her bedroom door to the bed. "I'll be right back."

"Don't be long." Grant swished his hand across the spot on the bed where she'd just been. "I'd like a replay of last night before I go."

"Which part? There's no way there's time for all of it."

"So we start and see how far we get."

Tara smiled, but a wave of goose bumps raced across the surface of her skin. Grant had always been sexy and fun, but she hadn't banked on how different he would be in bed. She never, ever would have guessed that there was a growling alpha beneath that quiet exterior. The doorbell rang again and she rushed down the stairs. "I'll be there in a minute." Tara arrived in the foyer and plucked last night's heels from the floor, chucking them into the front closet. She flipped the dead bolt for the front door, amazed she'd had the presence of mind to lock it. Grant had been all consuming and he'd wasted no time getting things started.

She opened the door and her mouth fell open. *Astrid.*

"Good morning, Tara," Astrid said, snoopily peering inside.

Tara left the door open only a sliver. "Astrid. What are you doing here?"

"I thought I'd drop by and say hello."

This was all kinds of strange. It was seven in the morning and Astrid lived downtown. Why had she decided to turn up at Tara's door on a lark? "I'm about to get ready for work, so now's not a good time. I'm sorry. Maybe we could grab lunch sometime soon?"

"I haven't heard from you about my position at Sterling. I've been waiting and there's been nothing."

Dammit. No, Tara hadn't pushed Grant on the question of where Astrid would fit within the company structure. "I'm sorry. It's been a crazy week. Just trying to get settled and everything."

"That's great for you, but I own just as much of the company as you do, and I feel like I'm being left behind. If we're going to do this, I need to be included. Right now, I'm just sitting in my apartment all day long. It isn't fair."

These were all valid points. Tara had promised Astrid a role and she'd done nothing about it. She needed to get her act together or this was all going to fall apart. Astrid could do anything she wanted with her share of the company…like sell it to someone who had no interest in keeping Grant and Tara in their positions. "I'm genuinely sorry. I'll talk to Grant and we'll get something worked out."

"He's upstairs, isn't he?"

The air was knocked right out of Tara's lungs. She wanted to construct a cover for what was going on, especially since it was never going to happen again, but she couldn't lie. She didn't have it in her. She opened the door a little wider. "How did you know?"

"I was at the game last night. I couldn't sit in my apartment for another night. The kiss cam? You two really went for it. It was almost like this has been going on for some time." Astrid pressed her camera-ready lips together, playing coy.

"It hasn't. At all."

Astrid shrugged, but it was apparent she didn't believe Tara's answer. "Well, whatever. I followed my hunch and drove over this morning. As soon as I saw Grant's car in front of your house, I knew I was right."

Tara's neighbor Britney with the sensitive dog was standing out on the sidewalk, watching Tara's exchange with Astrid. Just what Tara didn't need—more people talking. Tara had to take away the show. "Do you want to come in?" she asked Astrid.

"I thought you'd never ask." Astrid stepped across the threshold.

Tara closed the door behind her, struggling to come to terms with this turn of events. She was always so careful about things like discretion, but she hadn't ever had someone as shrewd as Astrid watching her. There was no question now that things with Grant could not continue. They could not be sleeping together while he was in charge at Sterling and she was carving out her niche. It was stupid of her to think for even a moment that it might work. She'd let her desire for him overshadow everything that was truly important—her new career, her rightful place at Sterling and her chance to finally stop waiting to be happy. Work made her happy. Not men. That had been proven time and again in her life. Aside from any of that, she'd promised Miranda and Astrid that she would make this work for *all* of them. She'd been entirely too focused on herself.

Tara led Astrid into the kitchen and made her a quick cappuccino with the professional machine she'd had installed when renovating the kitchen. "Do you want to go sit out on the balcony? It's a beautiful morning. I'll only be a minute."

"Tell Grant I say hi," Astrid quipped before sliding the glass door open and letting in a rush of sea air.

You'll probably get to tell him yourself. "I'll be right back."

Tara took her time walking to her bedroom, carefully composing her thoughts. She didn't want to hurt Grant's feelings, but Astrid's arrival was her wake-up call. She'd made promises to her and Miranda, and she had a duty to perform at Sterling. Being involved with Grant stood in direct opposition to that. Drawing in a deep breath for confidence, she opened the door and slipped inside, discovering that Grant was getting dressed.

"I forgot that I have a meeting at the office at nine. I really do need to get home and grab a shower." He shook out his shirt and threaded his arms through the sleeves.

"We have a problem."

"I wanted to spend more time with you, too, but I can't blow off this meeting."

"That's not what I mean. Astrid is here. She was at the game last night. She saw the kiss. There's no telling who else saw it." She didn't want to be so annoyed by something as silly as a kiss cam, but she was. If it hadn't happened, if they hadn't gone to the game at all, they wouldn't be in this situation. Then again, something told her that she and Grant might have found another excuse to fall into bed. Their attraction was that incendiary.

"I didn't even think about that." Grant furrowed his brow. "This is not good."

She nodded. "No kidding. What are we going to say if someone calls us on it?"

"Honestly? I have no idea. I mean, it was a pretty hot kiss."

Incredibly hot. Just thinking about it sent a shudder through Tara. But she didn't have time for that. Not now. "We have to tell people it meant nothing." Tara gestured to the bed, where the sheets were rumpled and the comforter twisted and piled. "Just like we have to tell each other that this meant nothing. There's too much on the line."

Grant cast a look at the site of their tryst. "I agree. It was impulsive. We obviously weren't thinking straight."

Apparently Tara had hoped for at least a little resistance from Grant. Why else was she feeling so utterly disappointed by his agreement that they'd made a mistake? "I don't think you can say that about everything last night. I got you to agree to move forward with the Seaport project. We were both thinking straight when that conversation happened."

Grant buttoned his shirt, shaking his head. "That's all that really matters, isn't it?"

"What's that supposed to mean?" She greatly disliked his tone.

"It means that you took me out and flirted with me all night, then you kissed me at the baseball game. Now that it's the next day, I'm starting to think that the whole night was a campaign to butter me up. To get what you want out of me."

"Do you honestly think that?"

"We were both caught up in the moment. I got wrapped up in your vision and you got wrapped up in me saying yes to your ideas. It might not have been the best time to decide to sleep together." He stuffed the tails of his shirt into his pants and buckled his belt.

Something in Tara wanted to challenge Grant, but he wasn't wrong. She *had* been swept away by him taking her seriously. It was so validating. "In the meantime, what do we do about Astrid? I can't lie and tell her nothing happened." Tara sat on the bed, her mind scrambling for a way to deal with Astrid.

"She's not stupid. You know that."

"Of course."

"We need to convince her to keep this to herself.

She owns a sizable piece of Sterling and this could damage the company. Therefore, she needs to keep it quiet. Which I mean, is the only fair thing, anyway. We're consenting adults—it was a one-time thing. Time for all of us to move on."

A one-time thing. Tara had thought that at one point last night, but that was before they'd arrived back at her house and he'd pinned her hands against the wall in the foyer. Just like the moment out on the promenade, that made her see him differently. She'd even gone to sleep with nothing more than thoughts of wanting more from him. But maybe she'd been delirious from orgasms. "So we'll go talk to her now?"

Grant shook his head and pulled on his socks, then stuffed his feet into his shoes. "I think this is all on you. You three are the ones who made the decision to band together. I don't want it to be seen as me interfering if I say something to her. But I do want you to make it clear to her that she needs to stay quiet."

The only trouble was that Astrid had a mind of her own. There was no telling what she might do or say if it benefitted her in any way. "It'll make my job a lot easier if I can tell her when and where she should report to work. She's mad that an entire week has gone by and she's been sitting in her apartment with nothing to do."

"Tell her I'll call her this afternoon. She can start on Monday." Grant glanced in the mirror and straightened his shirt. Tara was taken aback by the change in his demeanor. A switch had been flipped.

He was no longer sweet, fun and sexy Grant, nor was he the take-charge man she'd slept with. He was all business and all too ready to distance himself from her. About to leave, he held out his hand. "Thanks for a nice night, Tara."

"A handshake? Seriously?"

He cocked an eyebrow at her, which felt like he was telling her she was an idiot for asking. "We're back to being colleagues and nothing else. It's probably for the best."

"It's just us in this room. You can at least give me a hug."

"Honestly, I think a hug will make this more difficult."

Tara choked back a sigh and shook Grant's hand. "Got it, boss. I'll see you in a little bit." She leaned against the doorway as he strode down the hall and escaped into the stairwell. The sound of the front door closing a minute later confirmed that he was gone.

Tara wasn't sure what she was feeling right now. Regret came to mind, but as for what she wished she hadn't set in motion, she wasn't sure. Had this idea to bring the wives together and shoehorn themselves into Sterling been a stupid idea? Or was Grant the poor choice? She didn't want to slap that label on either of her decisions, but she knew that she couldn't have it both ways. She couldn't have this powerful new job *and* Grant. And since she knew that her compatibility with Grant in bed was zero predictor of anything beyond sex, she needed to get back on track. She needed to get back into Astrid's good graces.

After throwing on a pair of yoga pants and a light sweater, Tara grabbed a cup of coffee and went out to the balcony. Astrid was reading something on her phone, but she quickly tucked it inside her purse.

"Sorry about that," Tara said.

"I saw Grant leave. I decided to be discreet and not yell goodbye."

"Thanks." Tara curled up in the chair next to Astrid. "Last night was a mistake. And it won't happen again. I told Grant as much. I think he and I had some issues to work out. Stuff from before Johnathon and I were together. But it's all over now. I don't want you to worry about it. I'm also hoping we can count on your discretion."

Astrid sipped her coffee, staring ahead at the ocean. "Sure. As long as I get the right job within the company."

There was no mistaking the implied threat. "Of course. Grant said he'd call you this afternoon and you can start on Monday. It looks like we're moving ahead with the Seaport Promenade project, so hopefully you can be involved with that. We can work together on it."

Astrid smiled, which made Tara feel slightly better, although she still wasn't sure she could trust her completely. "Sounds good. I'll look forward to hearing from Grant."

"Everything else okay?" Tara asked.

"For the most part, yes. I spoke to Miranda yesterday."

"You did?" Tara wished she didn't sound so flabbergasted, but she was.

"I called to see how she's doing."

"That was nice of you." Honestly, it was astounding of her.

"I don't want things to be so strained between us." Astrid tucked herself farther back in the chair. "I'm sure this sounds crazy, but it feels like she's one of the only connections I have to Johnny. I'm having such a hard time coming to terms with his death."

They were each struggling in their own way. "That makes a lot of sense. She was certainly more connected than most of us when he died."

"And she was there when he passed. I can't explain it, but I feel tied to her. Also, I'm trying to tamp down my envy over the baby. I told myself that if Miranda and I became close, maybe it would help me be more purely happy about it." She took a sip of her coffee. "I also talked to my therapist over the phone earlier this week. She helped me through some of this."

Maybe I need to talk to a therapist, too. Tara admired Astrid's willingness to be kind to Miranda. It had to be difficult for her. But it also confounded Tara a bit. Between the pregnancy and the revelation that Johnathon had not told Astrid he'd married a third time, Tara had only envisioned those two having problems. And she couldn't help but think about the unstable nature of a group of three people sharing the same interest. Alliances would naturally form, and if the one between Miranda and Astrid became especially strong, that would leave Tara out in the cold.

"Is that crazy?" Astrid asked. "Telling myself that getting close to Miranda will make me less jealous?"

It was then that Tara heard the utter heartbreak in Astrid's voice. It was clear as the morning air, and just as strong as the sun. The loss she felt over her inability to conceive with Johnathon was still front and center. It might follow her for the rest of her life. It was only natural that she'd seek some way to come to terms with it. It was certainly a healthier approach than living in denial, or worse, allowing herself to be angry.

Tara set aside her coffee cup and leaned forward in her chair, reaching for Astrid's hand. "I don't think it's crazy. I think it's admirable. I think it's very big of you to set aside your own hurt and support Miranda right now. Frankly, I need to do more to reach out to her and see if she needs anything."

"I'm sure she'd like to hear from you."

Tara let go of her hold on Astrid and sat back. "Maybe the three of us could have dinner one night. That could be fun." She could hardly believe what was coming out of her mouth—the idea of the three of them seeing each other in a social setting of their own planning would have been entirely implausible a few weeks ago.

"I like that idea. Plus, it'll give me something to do."

"I'll get going on that. I've just been so distracted this week."

"By Grant?"

Tara shook her head. She'd made a huge mistake by letting the heat between Grant and her get in the way of the goals she had with Sterling and the promises she'd made to the other wives. In many ways, her conversation with Astrid only confirmed how far she'd strayed off the path and how she needed to get back on it quickly. "No. I swear that won't happen again. I'm focused on we three wives getting the most out of our stake in Sterling. That's all I care about right now."

"Good. Because I'm ready to get to work. First thing Monday morning."

Nine

Grant drove a little too fast getting home. He didn't care about rules or limitations or, apparently, traffic laws right now. Frustration was grinding away inside his head, filtering down into his body and getting entirely too comfortable. How could last night with Tara go so spectacularly only to have everything fall apart this morning? Damn Astrid and her amateur sleuthing. Damn that stupid kiss cam.

And there in the back of his head was the real thing that was bothering him—why did everything he touched seem to go just ever-so-slightly off the rails? Was this a sign of what was to come now that he was at the helm of Sterling? Because Johnathon never had a problem running the company and he'd certainly never seemed to have a problem with women, especially Tara. Yes, their marriage had ended, but he'd been the one to cut it off. He had three years of wedded bliss with her and a good year before that. Grant would've gladly taken that time with her. He would've taken a fraction of it.

Grant pulled into one of three garage bays at his home in La Jolla, perched up on a cliff overlooking the Pacific. He turned off the ignition, drew in a deep, cleansing breath and knew he had to find a way to win out over his own inner struggle. His heart and body had been greedy last night. Tara was right there, breathtaking and bold, everything he'd ever wanted in a woman, and everything that wasn't his to have. And so he'd gone there. He'd stomped on loyalty. He'd slept with the woman who had once been his best friend's wife, the woman who he also had to run Sterling Enterprises with. It was as stupid a choice as he could have made. He had to own that.

He strode into the house, his big empty showplace. It was modern and minimalist, and situated in one of the most enviable settings in the world, windswept but pristine, with the untamed cobalt ocean at its feet. It was everything he could ever want in a home. Except that it was also a multimillion-dollar testament to his unwanted bachelorhood. He didn't want to be the sole inhabitant. He'd never wanted it that way. Hope had always been in the back of his head, or perhaps in the center of his heart. He'd always thought he'd meet the right woman, get married and have children. He'd even envisioned little ones riding tricycles or kicking a ball through these expansive halls, across the wood floors that cost a fortune, quite possibly ruining them, and Grant not caring at all. Sure, it was traditional and not terribly original, but it was his true desire. Coming from a loving family and having four siblings might make for dull cocktail-party conversation, but he'd always been thankful for it. In this high-stakes, big-money world he lived in, those roots kept him grounded.

In his bedroom, he took off his clothes, forcing himself to throw them in the hamper destined to go to the cleaners. His shirt held the faintest traces of Tara's beguiling scent. It was going to be hard enough to breathe it in at work. He didn't need to torture himself with it.

He climbed into the shower, lathering up his chest and attempting to scrub away the remnants of last night. The hot spray wasn't doing nearly enough to help him shake off the effects of Tara. He was twice torn, between what was and what should have been—the business he'd helped build was now at his command, but if that fateful moment hadn't happened on the golf course, Johnathon would've been here to lead the way instead. He never would have had last night with Tara. He didn't want to regret it, but how could part of him not? He couldn't ignore the feeling that he had betrayed his best friend by taking Tara to bed. It didn't matter that Johnathon wasn't here anymore. He wouldn't have liked it if he was. And Grant truly wished his best friend was still alive. For all of Johnathon's faults, Grant still missed him. He missed talking to him every day, reining him in at his more erratic moments and marveling at his brilliant ones. He missed having a true partner in this business that was all consuming. The two of them had been through so much together. It was impossible to turn his back on the memories.

He had to hustle to get back to the office before nine. As he strolled out of the elevator and into the reception area, his stomach sank. The full staff wasn't in yet, but it was still entirely too quiet. There was an unmistakable air in the office. There were whispers and glances. The office grapevine was just as aware of Astrid's findings as he'd feared—they all knew about the kiss cam. They knew about the very real heat between Tara and him.

Roz the office receptionist was unpacking her bag. "Good morning, Mr. Singleton." She eyed him with suspicion as he walked past.

"Morning," he replied, doing his best to act as though nothing was going on. Still, a walk down the hall told him that his wariness was warranted. People knew about the kiss and they were talking about it. It was now his job to squash that as quickly as possible. That started with keeping Tara in the office on the opposite end of the building. He needed as little proximity as they could get away with. It was too dangerous. He knew how tempted he was by her.

He sat at his desk and his assistant checked in with him a few minutes later. If she knew what was going on, she didn't let on, and that was a relief. Perhaps the rumors could die quickly. Unfortunately, Tara showed up in his doorway several minutes later, looking like a dream in a sleek red dress that showed off her curves and her legs. It was appropriate for the office, but it was still as sexy as anything Grant had ever seen. He truly wished he could go for five minutes without being tested.

She knocked on the door frame. "Do you have a minute? We need to talk."

"Sure." His body immediately responded to her presence. It felt like every hair on his head was standing straight up. Everything below his waist went tight.

Tara took a step inside and went to close the door.

"Leave it open," he blurted, bolting out of his seat.

Tara cast him a questioning look. "What's up?"

"Everyone knows," he whispered.

"I realize that. Precisely why I'd like to close the door. So we can have some privacy."

A deep grumble left his throat. He hated playing these games, especially at work. It was not the way he liked to do things. He was supposed to be the guy with nothing to hide. "No. Leave it open. If there's anything we can't discuss with the door open, we shouldn't be talking about it at all. At least not here."

"Fine." Tara marched to one of the armchairs opposite his desk and sat. "There are three things we need to talk about. Astrid, the Seaport Promenade and my office move."

She wasn't making this any easier on him. "I think we make Astrid the project coordinator for the Seaport. You can oversee her work," Grant said.

"Do you really think she'll go for that? She owns just as much of the company as I do."

"And you have experience in this realm. She does not. She'll learn a lot by doing this, and quite frankly, I think it'll help her decide if this is something she really wants to do long term. I'm not convinced she's cut out for this."

Tara pursed her lips, but nodded in agreement. "Okay. You'll call her and let her know?"

"Yes." He only hoped Astrid wouldn't give him crap about what happened last night. "As for the project itself, it should be obvious that I'm committed to us submitting a proposal and bid to the city. I'd like to assign Clay Morgan as lead architect. He has background in designing public spaces, he's incredibly smart and well suited to working within the constraints the city sets. I think he'd be perfect."

"Interesting."

"What?" Grant disliked Tara's leading tone. He was doing his best to make this work, when really all he wanted to do was shut the door and get her to take off that red dress.

"It feels a little bit like you're setting up Astrid for failure. She and Miranda are still working on their differences, but you saw the way they talked to each other in the lawyer's meeting. I could see them returning to that dynamic at any time. Miranda and her brother are extremely close. Do you not see a potential problem there?"

"And do you want to give Astrid a job or not?"

Tara leaned back in her chair and surveyed the view through his doorway, presumably looking to see if anyone might overhear what she was about to say. "We have to. Not only because of her shares of the company, but because it might be the only way we can keep her from talking."

"I think we need to be able to keep tabs on her, too. We can't simply hand her something and let her run with it. She's an unknown quantity right now."

"That's fair."

"I realize this isn't ideal, but I'm doing my best, okay?" Grant felt a headache starting to brew, right in the center of his forehead. His shoulders were tightening. Not a great way to start a Friday, especially when he knew that he had a long, frustratingly lonely weekend ahead of him.

"I know you are. I'm sorry. I'm sorry everything got so messy."

"Yeah, well, so am I. You were right about what you said earlier this morning. It was a mistake." Those last four words had barely left his mouth, and he couldn't help but want to take them back. They were the right thing to say, but damn it all if they didn't feel wrong. He'd dreamed for so many years of being with Tara. He hated that the memory of their one night together was now tainted by everything that had happened since then.

"Right. Of course. Not to be repeated."

"Exactly." That was that then—the beginning and end of Grant and Tara had transpired in fewer than twenty-four hours.

"If we're back to focusing on work, I have to ask about next steps with Seaport."

Grant shuffled some papers on his desk, desperate to hide his wounded pride. "Run with it and keep me apprised. You have your team—Astrid, Clay and Sandy. It's your project to bring together."

Tara shifted in her seat and recrossed her legs. His stupid eyes were drawn to them the way a horse is drawn to cool water. Those beautiful stretches of her skin had been wrapped around him last night. And he couldn't have that happen again. "That's it then?" she asked.

He was trying so hard to keep it together right now. He did want to close the door to his office. He wanted to take her into his arms and kiss her exactly like he'd been brave enough to do last night. "That's it. Green light from me. Go ahead and prove me wrong."

"Okay. I will." She got up from her seat and stepped closer to his desk. "One more thing before I go. What about my office? We can't work together closely when I'm so far away."

Distance would help him keep his head straight. It would help him focus on big-picture projects at Sterling and let Tara do her thing. He hoped they could peacefully coexist. They had to. Or he had to find a way to raise the capital to buy her, Miranda and Astrid out of their chunk of the company. At this point, he was going to have to offer them far more than the shares were worth, a reality he found especially grating. The value was something he'd created. He didn't want to have to pay for it. "Considering what happened last night, and the fact that Astrid knows about it, as well as most of the office, I think it's in our best interest to keep you where you are."

She folded her arms across her chest, which only served to frame her bustline in a too-pleasing way. "I don't want this to be a long-term answer."

"We can re-evaluate in a month. The office chatter will only get worse if you move into the office next to mine. I also think that for the time being, we should keep our talks to email as much as possible. Avoid being seen together." He dared to look her in the eye, wanting to underscore his seriousness. Too bad he hated having to say it. "That's my decision, okay?"

"Hmm. Exercising some authority?"

"As a matter of fact, I am. I still know what's best for the company."

Tara knocked her knuckle on Grant's desk. "I guess you're right. It doesn't mean I like it."

Sandy appeared at Grant's door. He was happy for the interruption. "Ms. Sterling, the other Ms. Sterling is on the phone for you. Astrid."

Grant had to laugh at that, although he did it under his breath. There were far too many Ms. Sterlings in his orbit right now. And for the moment, one of them—Tara—needed to circle as far away from him as possible.

The weekend came and went with little rest, as Tara spent most of it deep in thought over everything that had happened since Johnathon's death. And in some instances, everything that came before it. She'd even scrounged around in a storage closet and found an old photo album from the time when she'd been married to Johnathon. Many of the pictures were from the lavish vacations they took, all of which were made with Grant and his girlfriend at the time, which was never the same. They rented a sprawling villa in Tuscany one autumn, where they drank wine for days, toured art museums and spent hours sunning themselves by the pool. There was the chalet perched atop a mountain in Switzerland, a getaway filled with endless ski runs and nights devoted to conversation in front of the fire.

Quite possibly the most memorable trip was to Costa Rica. Grant had hunted down a two-bedroom, two-bath treehouse tucked up into the rainforest canopy. That had been a grand adventure. They went on zip-line tours, swam in natural pools under waterfalls and sat on the porch for hours, sipping rum and watching the antics of the howler monkeys and macaws. Tara realized that she and Grant had taken most of the pictures from these vacations, which meant she was stuck trying to remember the names of these random women he'd brought along as his companions. She couldn't recall a single one. When Grant and Johnathon were in the frame together, their genuine connection was always there. They had been like brothers, which was such a gift for Johnathon—he and his own brother had always had a contentious relationship.

Tara had to wonder if that was part of what had made Grant so eager to step away from her the other morning. Setting aside the obvious conflict of their working relationship, and what had been the immediate threat of Astrid telling everyone she knew that Grant and Tara had slept together, perhaps it was Grant's history with Johnathon that made him second-guess what they'd done. Grant was in a far different situation than Tara—his allegiance to Johnathon had gone right up until the moment he'd died. Much of Tara's went away when he filed for divorce. It wasn't the same. And perhaps she needed to give Grant some credit for not wanting to violate the trust that had come with his brotherly bond with Johnathon. Things like that didn't simply dissolve when someone passed away.

As she drove to work on Monday morning, it occurred to her that there might be something else going on here—perhaps she had underestimated Grant. Not only in the bedroom, but in the sphere of work. He'd shown himself as nothing less than a formidable man. He was not to be messed with. He'd also made it obvious that his allegiance was to Sterling Enterprises above all else. As to how much that was wrapped up in his friendship with Johnathon, she didn't know. But still, the fact that he'd taken Tara to bed wasn't about to slow him down with staking his claim on Sterling. And now she was in the position of having to stay away from him, when the reality was that he'd done nothing less than pique her interest by making love to her.

But sex would solve nothing. *Stay on your path, Tara. Get back to work.*

When she arrived at the office, she found Astrid in reception, looking absolutely stunning in a gray wool pencil skirt and black turtleneck. On anyone else, it would've looked a little too prim for the modern workplace. On Astrid, it was jaw-dropping.

"You ready to get to work?" Tara asked.

"Absolutely."

Tara guided Astrid through the maze of halls, passing her office, so she could lead Astrid to the one she'd be occupying. "This will be where you'll be working for the time being. Everything's in a state of flux right now, so I don't think this is where you'll end up permanently. I know it's maybe not quite as nice as you might have wanted." Tara braced for commentary on the small and spartan nature of the space. Astrid was accustomed to luxury and the finest of everything.

"This will work fine. I don't need a fancy office. I just need a place to sit and a desk. The window is nice." Astrid offered a quick smile, seeming satisfied.

Tara admired Astrid's willingness to go with the flow. She hadn't expected it, at all. Johnathon had always painted Astrid as being incredibly high-maintenance, the sort of woman who needed constant attention and adulation. That hadn't been Tara's experience thus far. Astrid certainly had a flair for high drama—showing up at the first meeting of the wives dressed as Widow of the Year, and then again turning up at Tara's house and busting her on her tryst with Grant. But as for being needy, Astrid seemed nothing less than self-sufficient.

"You'll be working on the Seaport Promenade project with me," Tara said. "Since you're just getting started in the world of development, Grant thought it best for us to work together so I and a few other key people in the office can show you the ropes."

Astrid nodded eagerly and tucked her long blond hair behind her ear. "Yes, of course. I'm ready to learn."

Yet again, Tara was pleasantly surprised. Astrid might have owned seventeen percent of the company, but she sure wasn't acting as though she was entitled to anything other than an opportunity. "Great. Let's go chat with Clay Morgan, the lead architect on the project. I can explain everything to you on our way down to his office."

Astrid reached for Tara's arm, her face now painted with concern. "He's Miranda's brother, isn't he?"

"He is. But you and Miranda have started to iron things out, haven't you?"

Astrid nodded. "Yes. But I'm still not sure she likes me."

Tara patted Astrid on the arm, wanting to reassure her. "She's been through a lot. We've all been through a lot. All the more reason for us to have that dinner together. Does Friday still work for you?"

"It does. I wouldn't miss it."

"Great."

The two women strode down the hall to the suite where the architects' offices were. She loved this part of the Sterling operation. It made her think of her dad, and his dreams. He would've been excited to see so many talented people hard at work. He'd always hoped to find himself in a place exactly like this, but he'd never reached that goal. All the more reason for Tara to keep striving for more in this new phase of her professional life. She wasn't waiting to be happy. She was making her dad proud by going for it.

Tara reached Clay's door, which was wide open. Inside, Clay was hard at work at his drafting table. In the background, classical music played, but at a volume so low that it was hardly audible. Tara had met Clay a few times, and if she had to stick him with a label, it would have been *intense*. His hair was very dark, nearly black, just like Miranda's. It was longish on top, and he was always threading his fingers through it, flopping it from one side to the other. His blue eyes were so dark that they sometimes looked like midnight. He was tall and broad, but quiet and reserved. There always seemed to be quite a lot going on under the surface.

Tara hated to interrupt him, especially when he was so hard at work, but she had to make this introduction. She rapped on his door quietly. He looked up at her with those stormy eyes, but he seemed to quickly see past Tara to Astrid. Tara was accustomed to this response from men when she was with Astrid. The woman had graced hundreds of magazines and the runway for a reason—she was breathtakingly beautiful.

"Clay. Hi," Tara started. "I wanted to introduce you to Astrid Sterling. She's going to be project manager on the Seaport project. You and Grant talked about it, right?"

He took a quick survey of his workspace, which was littered with pencils and large sheets of drafting paper. "Yeah. Sure. I'm sorry. I would've cleaned up if I'd known you were coming."

Astrid walked past Tara and helped him with the pencils. "It's okay. I'm good at straightening up."

Clay was a proverbial deer in the headlights, not saying a thing and frozen in place. Men did all sorts of strange things in Astrid's presence. "Please. Don't." He stopped Astrid by clapping his hand down on hers. He'd apparently snapped back to attention.

Astrid shook off the rebuff, but her cheeks were red with embarrassment. "I'm so sorry."

"It's okay. I just like to have my office a certain way."

Tara was eager to diffuse the sudden tension in the air. "So, Clay, as you know, Grant wants you as lead architect on the project. Astrid will be learning along the way and managing the day-to-day. I'll be dealing with the city, with help from my assistant, Sandy."

Clay picked up one of the pencils from his desk and rattled it back and forth between his fingers. "I've already done my own research on the specs. We're behind the eight ball. The first plans are due in five weeks. If we don't pass the initial phase, we're out of the running. And my workload is already considerable, so this is going to be a big challenge."

Tara decided that getting Clay on her side was of paramount importance. Grant would think she couldn't handle things if Clay went complaining to him about the timeline or the project in general. "You have a daughter, right?"

Clay's eyes narrowed. "I do. She's five."

"One of my prime objectives in our version of the project is to make it more kid friendly. There's not enough for families downtown. I think your knowledge based on that alone is crucial."

"There are other dads in the department."

"But none who are doing it all on their own as a single dad. I'm guessing you bring a specific set of ideas to the equation. Plus, Grant swears up and down that you're the top architect in the firm. I want the best for this project."

Clay pursed his lips, the pencil still wagging in his hand. "Okay. We need to have a planning meeting as soon as possible. A site visit. I'd like to hear some ideas outside of my own. It's important to have more than one perspective."

"That's perfect because I have lots of ideas. Grant really seemed to like them." Just thinking about presenting her ideas to Grant was making her sad about the other night. They'd both been so caught up in the moment, feeding off each other's enthusiasm. It had felt only natural that they'd ended up in bed together, and in the moment, it had been so right. She and Grant fit together like two puzzle pieces. But that was not to be. She had to stay focused on what was ahead of her.

"Okay. Sounds good," Clay said.

Tara breathed a sigh of relief. "Fantastic. I'll have Sandy bring you the official specs this afternoon. Perhaps we can meet first thing tomorrow morning?"

"That works," Clay said.

"Is this your daughter in the picture?" Astrid asked, picking up a frame from the credenza.

"It is. She was a flower girl when my sister and Johnathon got married."

Astrid admired the photograph and Tara stole a glance over her shoulder. Clay was standing next to bride Miranda with his arm around her. Clay's daughter was in a pretty pink dress with a basket of flowers. It made Tara's heart ache to think about how happy everyone was in that photograph, but it also made her equally sad to think about what Astrid must be thinking while looking at it. She hadn't been told that Johnathon had remarried. This was a piece of history she'd only recently learned of.

"When was the wedding?"

"Late May last year. Memorial Day weekend. They were barely married for a year. It's so sad," Clay answered.

"Was it a short engagement?" Astrid asked.

Tara found the question odd. Why would Astrid want to know these details? "A few months, I guess," Tara answered.

"Sounds right to me," Clay added.

Astrid tapped her finger against the frame, then promptly put the photograph down and made for the door. "Thanks, Clay," she said, hardly looking at him before she disappeared into the hall.

"Is she okay?" Clay asked.

Tara didn't know the answer to that question, but she had a good idea. "I'm sure she's fine. Thanks for letting us steal some of your time today."

"Yeah. Of course."

Tara rushed out into the hall. She expected that she'd have to chase after Astrid, but she was just outside the door, leaning against the wall with her face buried in her hands.

"Come on," Tara said, urging her ahead with a gentle tug of her arm. "Let's you and I get some privacy." She and Astrid filed into the ladies' room.

"Was it the photo from Johnathon's wedding to Miranda?"

"Yes." Astrid's voice was soft and unsteady.

"I'm sorry you had to see that, but maybe it's better that it finally happened. You and Miranda are becoming friends. It was only a matter of time before she invited you over one night."

Astrid braced her hands on the bathroom counter, staring into the mirror and shaking her head. She wasn't tearful, but the color was definitely gone from her face. "I can't believe it."

"Believe what?"

Astrid looked Tara right in the eye via her reflection. "Johnathon cheated on Miranda."

"Wait. What? How do you know?"

Astrid turned around and crossed her arms over her chest, leaning back against the vanity. "I know because he cheated on her with me."

Ten

Tara cursed her ex-husband for days. Nearly an entire work week, to be exact. *Damn you, Johnathon.* How could he have done that? Sleep with one ex-wife weeks before marrying the next one? It was unconscionable. It was also a little crazy that Tara had such a burning desire to find out why he'd done it. *Leave it alone*, she kept telling herself. But she couldn't.

Tara had a vested interest in keeping this secret buried, even if it killed her to play a part in Johnathon's misdeeds. If Miranda found out and blew up over it, the wives' majority interest in the company would be compromised. There was no telling what either Astrid or Miranda would do in that situation, but Tara could imagine some terrible scenarios. They might feel pitted against each other and sell to one of the other shareholders, leaving Tara with very few options. If they sold to Grant, it would be game over. Tara would lose her chance to run the company. Miranda and Astrid might even band together against Tara. Crazier things had happened.

The wives needed to be a unified front, but beneath the surface, things were beginning to splinter. First there was the pregnancy and now, the infidelity. Beyond that, Tara was responsible for some of the uneven ground they were walking on. It had been foolish to sleep with Grant. It had been shortsighted to allow herself to get caught up in the moment and give in to those carnal desires, and her own deep-seated curiosity about what it might be like to sleep with him. She couldn't beat herself up about it though. She refused to do that. He rocked her world a week ago. On some level, it had been worth it.

For now, her most pressing problem was that Astrid would not stop asking Tara if she thought Grant knew about the infidelity. It bothered Astrid greatly, and she'd been unable to get a meeting with him. His schedule was ridiculously full. Tara kept putting Astrid off, but she couldn't do it forever. And it benefitted her to ask the question before Astrid had the chance to do it herself. If Astrid unleashed her anger on Grant in the office, Clay might find out about it and that would all lead back to Miranda. It was a risk to ask Grant, but she needed to do it. Luckily, she not only had access to his calendar, but she'd befriended his assistant.

She showed up at his office just as he was getting off a call. "Do you have a minute?" she asked.

"Sure," he answered, typing away at his keyboard.

Tara closed the door behind her. She couldn't let anyone hear their discussion. The rumor mill would gobble up this delicious morsel of gossip and it would spread like wildfire.

"Tara. We talked about this. About the door," he said.

"I know. But we need privacy." That one word—*privacy*—and the accompanying knowledge that they were now alone did a number on her. It made her face and chest flush with heat. It made her legs feel rubbery. Being in his presence heightened the memory of his touch. It boiled it down to a potent serum that streamed through her body. What would have happened if she and Grant hadn't had their hands forced the morning after? Would he have wanted more? Would she have agreed? She knew she would have. It would have been impossible to turn him down.

"The whole office will talk about it," he said.

"Let them talk. We have bigger fish to fry." Tara went to the window and looked out over the city skyline, her mind running too many disparate pieces of information at one time. Astrid. Johnathon. Miranda. It was such a mess. And it was time to crack it open. "You knew, didn't you?"

Grant sat back in his chair and crossed his legs. He'd removed his suit jacket at some point during the day, and rolled up the sleeves of his shirt. God, he had sexy forearms. Strong and long, with the perfect amount of dark hair. "Sorry. You're going to have to be a little more specific than that."

"Johnathon and Astrid. The real reason he never told Astrid about marrying Miranda."

Grant cleared his throat and averted his gaze. That told her all she needed to know, but she still wanted to hear it.

"Tell me," she said.

"I didn't find out about it until after the fact. I swear that if I had known ahead of time, I would have tried to talk him out of it."

"What happened?"

"I guess he just never had the nerve to tell Astrid when he met Miranda and they got involved. He couldn't bring himself to break her heart. He and Astrid still had a very on-again, off-again relationship after the divorce. She went back to Norway and he went there several times trying to reconcile."

This was news to Tara, and it hurt to hear it. Johnathon had no problem moving on after shuttling her out of his life. Astrid was on his arm in what felt like the blink of an eye. "I had no idea."

"It was heartbreaking, really. They both wanted children so badly, but they'd never been able to conceive. Years of trying and waiting every month and never having any luck took its toll on the marriage, but I think they still loved each other deeply."

Tara knew it had been rough for them, but she

hadn't been privy to the details. "What about after he and Miranda got engaged? That wasn't enough to keep him away from Astrid?"

"Apparently not. I thought he was flying to London to meet with a potential partner on a project. He didn't tell me he was stopping off in Norway on the way there."

"From what Astrid said, it was only weeks before the wedding. What prompted it?"

Grant shrugged. "You know what he was like. He sometimes simply let the wind carry him in one direction, even when he knew he should probably go the other way."

Tara did know that firsthand. She'd felt like that had been the case when Johnathon jettisoned her from Sterling and pushed her into real estate. It all happened so suddenly. One day she was working at their fledgling operation and the next, he was insisting she do something else and get her real estate license.

Grant pinched his nose and shook his head. "It's hard for me to know what was going through Johnathon's head at that point. All I know is that he went to Norway and he and Astrid slept together."

"He told you when he got back?"

"Actually, no. But he put some items from Norway on his expense report and he was out of the office when the folks in accounting asked me about it. Norway wasn't on his company itinerary, so they were checking to see if it was right."

"Did you confront him?"

"I did, and you can imagine how that went. There was no confronting Johnathon. He never wanted to own up to anything that made him look bad. He never wanted to appear human. He wanted everyone to love him unconditionally."

"And it worked for the most part."

"It did. He just made everyone else deal with his mistakes."

Tara knew that, too. When Johnathon had asked her to set aside her aspirations with Sterling, he'd told several people that it had been her choice to do so. That couldn't have been further from the truth, but Tara believed in a unified front when it came to marriage, and so she'd smiled and nodded and said that being a real estate agent had always been her dream. When it wasn't true.

"I don't really know what to do about this," she said, turning back to Grant. As she shifted, the sun steamed in through the window over her shoulder, first blinding her, then as her eyes adjusted, lighting him in a soft glow. It harkened back to their morning together and waking up next to him. It had been so lovely. He made her feel desired. Wanted. She hadn't felt that way in forever. Good God, she really wanted to kiss him again, to have his lips on the sensitive skin of her neck and feel his commanding hands all over her body. She really wanted to find out if their night together had been a fluke.

"You realize you're asking the wrong person,

right?" he asked. "I have every reason imaginable to stir up trouble between Astrid and Miranda. To divide your interests and hopefully convince one of you to sell."

"So why not create problems? You could have told either one of them about it and really driven the wedge between them. The opportunity was there from the moment Max told you he'd split Miranda's shares of the company between us." She didn't want to give him any ideas, but surely this had occurred to him.

"I could never do that. You should know that about me."

Tara drew in a deep breath. How did he manage to stay on the right side of everything? "I know, Grant. I know you're a good guy."

He shook his head and rose up out of his chair. "If it makes me a good guy because I want to win fair and square, then so be it. I guess I'm a good guy. Just please stop saying it like it's a bad thing. I realize that's not what you're attracted to. I guess you'd rather be with the sort of man who cheats on his new wife with his former one."

Ouch. "That's not what I'm attracted to."

"Then prove it to me."

Tara struggled to find a response. What was he saying? "With you?" The idea was all wrong. So why did it have to send such a tide of electricity through her body?

He shrugged and his eyes narrowed. "I don't know, Tara. You tell me."

Grant had nearly told her yes—prove it with him. Hell, he'd nearly come clean with a confession, but he wasn't ready. Something inside him was telling him to stay back. It was already hard enough to admit to himself that he'd been carrying a torch for Tara this whole time, even when she was married to his best friend. It would make him look weak and he didn't want Tara to see him that way. Yes, he'd been standing in Johnathon's shadow for years, but he'd been the backbone of the company and in many ways, he'd been that for Johnathon, too. It was just that nobody wanted to see it. The specter of Johnathon Sterling was too much for people to see past.

"No. I'm really not a good guy. At least not the way you're trying to put it." He stepped closer to her, scanning her face while memories of their night together gathered in his mind like storm clouds threatening torrential rain. He'd thought perhaps that last week might quench his desire for her, but it hadn't. Quite the opposite. She'd awoken something in him, a primal part of his psyche that wasn't willing to lose. Not anymore. He wanted what he wanted and he wasn't about to apologize for it.

"I really think this is a problem you need to rectify on your own, Grant."

She wasn't wrong. But he hoped she'd help him work it out. "I want you too much, Tara, and it's impacting my job. You're too beautiful. Too sexy. Too desirable. That's my real problem."

A crease formed between her eyes as doubt spread across her face. "Oh, please. I'm supposed to believe that you're so taken with me that you aren't still laser focused on the prize? You've always wanted to be at the helm of Sterling, and you're threatened by my presence. I don't think you can blame our battle of wills on attraction. No matter what you might have said to Johnathon over the years about being okay with playing second fiddle to him, I think you've always wanted Sterling first and foremost."

"You're not wrong. I have always wanted to be in charge. I was content in my role, but now that I've had a taste of the control it gives me, I'm not willing to pass up this opportunity." What he really wanted to say was that now that he'd had a taste of Tara, he wasn't willing to let her go. But she could turn on him so quickly, and there was more at stake than hurt feelings.

"Then we're at an impasse," she said. "I have a chance to fulfill my own dreams and I'm not willing to just shrug that off or walk away from it. No way. Not now. Not when I've got Astrid and Miranda and her baby counting on me to make the most of this."

"What happens if there's a rift between Astrid and Miranda? The truth has a way of coming out. Then where will you be, Tara? I know you're worried about them trusting you, but do you really, truly trust them?" It might sound like he was trying to sow discontent between the wives, but he wanted her to face the reality. Astrid and Miranda could turn on her at any point. And depending on which way they chose to go, whether they sold their shares to someone else or each other, it could all mean that control of Sterling would go into the wrong hands. It was a very real possibility. The sort of reality that kept Grant up at night.

"I have to trust that they'll keep up their end of the bargain. I have three months to prove that I can make this work, and we're barely two weeks in. Part of that is the Seaport project. If I can make that a success, I think I'll prove to them what I'm capable of."

Grant sighed as the weight of the situation he was in came crashing down around him once again. Any time he tried to shrug it off, it came roaring back. He wanted control, but so did Tara. He wanted Sterling to be successful, and Tara was on the same page, but in a markedly different way. And then there was this crazy side of himself that was rooting for Tara to realize her dreams, as well. Johnathon had held her back when he could, and it hadn't been fair. Grant cared about her too much for his own good.

"Where does this leave us?" Grant asked.

"The same place we were before I walked into your office. For now, we're on opposite sides of the same table. I want to run Sterling someday. I have to prove my worth to the wives and I need to prove myself to the staff. That means staying out of your bed."

"Technically, we were in *your* bed that night."

"You know what I mean."

"And is that what you really want, Tara? If you were being truly honest with yourself, and there were no repercussions, would you be saying that to me? To stay out of your bed?" He held his breath as he waited for the answer. If she was about to say yes, it would crush his most fragile dream, the one he had no business holding on to. But he wanted a dose of reality. It might help him see a way through this.

"I don't even know what you're asking, Grant. I don't do well with hypotheticals."

"That's not true. The woman who stood down at the waterfront and painted a picture for me with nothing more than her words and her passion is one-hundred-percent capable of seeing the possibilities."

"Are you asking me a question about business? Or us?"

Grant swallowed hard. He hadn't expected to meet this challenge today, to have to double down on what he wanted in his heart. But he had to say it, be done with it and let the dust settle. "I'm asking about us. The other night was spectacular and you know it. We have always had a connection. Don't tell me that years of flirting were for nothing. That there was nothing behind it. I don't believe that."

Tara waved him off and turned back to the window. "Well, of course I'm attracted to you, Grant. But do you really think that I will just throw away a professional opportunity so we can have a fling?

I'm not playing a short game here—I'm playing a long one."

"What makes you think it would only be short-term?"

"Two reasons. First off, you have never been able to make a relationship last for more than a month. Second, Sterling isn't going anywhere and we both want the same thing, which there is only one of."

If only Tara knew that the real reason he'd never been able to make a relationship work was because he compared all women to her. It was a stupid, fool-ish thing to do, and he'd fought it many times, but it always came down to that. Tara had a way of worm-ing her way back into his head. "What if we shared the leadership of Sterling?" He could hardly believe what he was suggesting. Johnathon would never have thought such a thing was a good idea, and Grant wasn't sure he thought it was smart, either. Still, he was looking for some fissure in the wall Tara had put up between them. There had to be a way in, a chink in her impenetrable armor.

She shook her head with such conviction that he braced for her answer. "No way. I want to win or lose, and really I just want to win. I should have had a role in this company all along. Johnathon should've kept me here. You know it, and I believe he knew it, too. There's no other reason for him to have written me into the will. I don't believe for a minute that he did it simply because he loved me like he loved As-trid and Miranda. I was a pit stop for him, and I paid a price for it. I got pushed off into a career I didn't want, and I got sidelined from the direction I wanted to take, which was to follow in my dad's footsteps. I have the chops, Grant. I know I do."

"I know. I know." He felt himself backing down, and he was tired of pushing himself into a corner. He had to accept that Tara's primary focus right now was on business. He was going to have to let her move forward with her plan. As long as she had the other wives on her side, they could call all the shots they wanted to. Hell, they could ouster him as CEO if they so chose. He couldn't play fast and loose with his role in the company. He had to learn his lesson. "So I guess I have my answer."

"I'd like to hear you say it just so I know we're on the same page," Tara said.

"We're fighting for control of Sterling Enterprises by seeing who can make the best leader. And that means that in the meantime, I'm staying out of your bed."

Eleven

Tara had offered to host dinner for Miranda and Astrid at her house, but Miranda had insisted they do it at her place. Balancing the pregnancy and her job had left her exhausted, and it was easier if she didn't have to go anywhere. Neither Tara nor Astrid had any reason to dispute her.

Tara pulled up to what had once been Miranda and Johnathon's home, now solely belonging to his widow. Situated in La Jolla, overlooking the water, this was close to Grant's home, which was a mile or two south. Grant and Johnathon had always been thick as thieves, and they'd liked being in close proximity. When Johnathon lived with Tara in Coronado, the two had always complained it was too far.

The house was truly magnificent, an absolute

showcase of Spanish architecture, with white stucco, black-leaded windows and a red clay roof topping the six different levels of the home. The tropical seaside landscape was lit up dramatically, as was the house, adorned with wrought iron carriage lamps. Tara had seen the property once, but that was before Johnathon and Miranda had bought it. She'd shown it to a couple five years ago, when the asking price was six million. Tara estimated that it had to be worth at least twelve by now. That was quite a nest egg for Miranda, on top of the millions Johnathon had left to her.

Financially, Miranda would do just fine. Emotionally, Tara didn't know, but she was sure she was about to find out how Miranda was faring.

Tara waited in her car in the driveway until Astrid arrived. She wanted the chance to speak to her for a moment before they went inside. Luckily, it was only a five-minute wait until Astrid zipped up in her little silver Porsche—a rental to keep her mobile while she was living in the city.

"You look absolutely gorgeous," Tara said, offering a hug.

"Thank you. You, too," Astrid replied. Tara felt as though it was more of an obligatory reply than anything.

"Before we go inside, I just wanted to say that I don't think it's a good idea to bring up what you told me the other day at work."

Astrid regarded Tara with utter horror. "What do

you take me for, Tara? A complete idiot? I would never do that."

Tara was taken aback. Astrid had been asserting herself in ways she hadn't expected. "I didn't mean any offense. I just wanted to be sure we could keep the peace. And I mean, what's done is done. Johnathon is gone. There's no one to answer for that particular misstep."

"I'm well aware that I can't yell and scream at him for that and neither can Miranda. I will have to carry that secret to my grave." She started off for the front door.

Tara followed, utterly relieved. "You're being remarkably calm about this."

Astrid checked her face in a compact mirror, then jabbed at the doorbell. "Vodka helps."

Tara smiled to herself, wondering why she'd bothered to worry about strife between the wives. They could find a way to make their peculiar partnership work. She felt certain of it. Well, reasonably sure. Money and business had a way of making everything more complicated.

Miranda answered and it was immediately apparent that she was not well. There was no glow of pregnancy. She had dark circles under her eyes and appeared pale and gaunt. Her normally gorgeous black hair was up in a messy bun, and she was wearing what appeared to be workout attire—gray yoga pants and a stretchy blue top. Tara was about to ask if they'd come at the wrong time, but Miranda put a quick end to that.

"Come on in." Miranda waved them both in to the two-story foyer, which had a sweeping staircase with an ornate scrolled railing and a spectacular wrought iron chandelier overhead. "I'm sorry I look like hell. Morning sickness is a misnomer. I'm having it all day long."

Astrid was quick to be at her side. "Do you need to sit down? Can I bring you anything?"

Tara found Astrid's attentiveness both sweet and odd. Perhaps Astrid was overcompensating. "Yes. Please. Let us know if we can do something. And we definitely don't have to eat. I can only imagine that the thought of being around food right now isn't particularly fun."

Miranda led them down a short hall and they emerged in the soaring great room, this space with a three-story-high ceiling and ringed with two levels of balconies. On the far side was a wall of windows overlooking the pool and beautifully landscaped yard, and up a half level was a gourmet kitchen, complete with eight-burner stove and Sub-Zero fridge. The house was even more of a showplace now than it had been the time Tara had seen it. Miranda had put her expert interior design touches on it, and she'd chosen very well, with sophisticated white sofas and splashes of color from throw pillows and modern art on the wall. Tara could only imagine what a nightmare it was going to be to babyproof this house, but that was a discussion for another day.

"My personal chef prepared dinner. I'm going to attempt to eat, but no promises." Miranda walked over to the bar. "Can I get either of you a drink?"

Tara was quick to assume bartender duties. "I can do this. It hardly seems fair that the woman who can't drink would have to make them. Astrid, what can I get you?"

"Vodka and soda, please," Astrid replied. Of course, she of zero body fat would choose the least caloric drink imaginable.

"Coming right up. And for you, Miranda?"

"Ginger ale, please. They should be in the fridge down below."

Tara quickly assembled the necessary supplies and delivered everyone's drinks. Astrid and Miranda had situated themselves at opposite ends of one sofa, leaving Tara to occupy the chair nearest Miranda. "So, I guess we should get the business part of our dinner meeting out of the way."

"Yes. I want to know what's going on. How's everyone in the office doing? I only get reports from Clay and he's not really up on office gossip," Miranda said.

"Generally, I think things are going really well. Everyone seems to be handling Johnathon's death as well as can be expected." Tara realized that the real reason morale at Sterling was good was all due to Grant's influence. She was the new person who'd interjected herself into this equation. Maybe her timing hadn't been the best, but she wasn't going to apologize for pursuing what had once been her dream and was now her dream again.

"I started this week," Astrid added. "I'm working with your brother, actually."

"Oh, interesting," Miranda said. "He didn't mention it."

There was a distinct stiffening of Astrid's posture as she took a healthy slug of her drink. Tara knew that Astrid wanted desperately to be taken seriously. All Tara could do to help with that was to put her in a position to prove herself. After that, it was all up to her.

"Yes. They're working on the Seaport Promenade project with the city. I think it will be a real boon if we can land it."

Miranda smiled quietly, seeming wistful as she took a sip of her ginger ale. "Johnathon really wanted to do that project. Grant fought him on it. Hard."

"I heard about that, but I think it's all worked out. We're moving forward with your brother as lead architect." Tara didn't want to mention that Grant's reasoning for staying out of it was because Johnathon had ruffled a lot of feathers with the city over the years. Miranda likely already knew about it, and if she didn't, Tara didn't want to disparage Johnathon. Miranda was carrying his baby, after all.

"Do you think there's a place for Johnathon's name in the project? There's going to be a park, isn't there? A place for children to play? Perhaps it could be the Johnathon Sterling Memorial Park. Or is there a fountain?"

Tara hadn't considered this idea at all. "There will be both, but I don't think we have any say in what they name anything. That's pretty much up to the city."

"Well, I think they should name something after him. Johnathon built half of the new buildings downtown. He's attracted businesses here. And he was a fixture of the community."

Tara looked to Astrid for help, but Astrid didn't say a peep. "I'll ask. That's really all I can promise right now." Tara hoped that was a diplomatic enough answer.

A timer in the kitchen began to beep. "That's dinner," Miranda said, slowly getting up from the sofa.

"Let me help." Tara followed her up to the open kitchen, which overlooked the great room. "What can I do?"

"I'm pregnant. I'm not an invalid." Miranda pulled a large sheet pan from the oven with parchment packets of something wonderful-smelling. She pulled three dinner plates from the cabinet and began piercing the paper bundles with a paring knife. "There's a salad in the fridge, if you can get that for me."

Astrid had joined them and was first to jump into action, leaving Tara to feel as though she was in the way. She brought over a large white ceramic bowl with elaborate relief work along the edges depicting fruit and vines. Everything Miranda chose was beautiful, and Tara silently told herself that she might need to up her game when it came to home decor.

The three of them went out to the patio by the pool, settling at a round scrolled iron table. Miranda's housekeeper had already set the table for them with exquisite silvery linens and water glasses. The meal was delicious—roasted red snapper with citrus and a touch of coconut milk, along with basmati rice. Miranda only picked at it, keeping her ginger ale close. The three shared polite conversation, but Tara couldn't ignore that it wasn't a natural thing for the three of them to be together. They'd all married the same man. They'd all had a very intimate relationship, good and bad, with Johnathon. They were as unlikely a trio of allies as could be.

It brought everything into focus. Not in theory, but in reality. Their arrangement was tenuous and Tara had better not count on any of this working out. Astrid's secret could come out and alienate Miranda forever. Astrid could decide that no one at Sterling would ever take her seriously and she could bail. And as for Tara, well, she was trying very hard at something she desperately wanted to be good at, but she wasn't quite there. Her decade in real estate might not have been her most loved, but at least she knew what she was doing, all the time, and she was exceptionally good at it. That just wasn't the case when it came to development.

Still, Tara had to cling to hope that things would

somehow work out for all three of them. Johnathon had brought them together for a reason, and despite his many faults, he was a very good judge of character. There had to be a common thread between them, one that went beyond their love for the same man. Tara was eager to find it. It would make their pact that much more solid. The first thing that came to mind for them to bond over was the baby.

"Miranda, have you started working on the nursery?" Tara set her dinner napkin across her plate. She wouldn't have brought this up in front of Astrid if she didn't think she could handle it. After all, it had been Astrid who'd reached out to Miranda. It was Astrid who'd wanted to forge a friendship.

"Are you kidding? I started picking stuff out the minute I found out I was pregnant. I just had it painted this week, but it's a work in progress."

"May we see it?" Astrid asked. Tara took that as confirmation that she could manage seeing the baby's room.

The three took their plates inside and left them on the kitchen counter, then Miranda led them to the central hall and up the stairs to the third floor. When they arrived at the landing, Tara remembered that this was the floor with the master bedroom, and it was to the right. Miranda led them to the left. Inside was a generous and quiet space, with butter-yellow walls and creamy-white carpet.

"I haven't picked out a crib yet. I don't want to

jinx myself." Miranda's hands went to her belly. "It's still so early."

Tara put her arm around Miranda's shoulders and gave her a squeeze. "There's no rush. You have plenty of time. It's a beautiful start though. I'm sure this room will be amazing when it's all done."

Astrid, who had yet to say a word or give any sign as to what she was feeling, wandered to the far side of the room, where a black-and-white photograph in a lovely white wood frame sat atop a small bookcase. She picked up the picture and looked at it, rubbing her thumb along the edge of the frame. When she looked up at Miranda and Tara, there were tears in her eyes. "Is this Johnny? When he was a boy?"

Miranda nodded and walked over to join Astrid. "It is. His brother Andrew sent it to me a few days ago. He was in town a week or so ago and came by the house."

Tara could hardly believe that Andrew had actually followed through and reached out to Miranda. And he'd visited her. That was a surprise. "Grant and I ran into him at a party."

"He told me," Miranda said. "I was glad that you and Grant asked him to contact me. This baby won't have a lot of family. Johnathon's parents are gone and so are mine. I have my brother and that's it. I hated that Andrew and Johnathon were at odds. And I think he already feels plenty bad about not having gone to the funeral."

"That was a big mistake on his part," Tara said.

"Yeah. I told him as much. I think the picture of Johnathon was his way of trying to say he was sorry."

"It's a beautiful gesture," Astrid said, still teary-eyed. "The baby can look at this and see what their dad looked like as a child."

The full weight of the situation seemed to settle over them, like a heavy blanket, muffling all sound and much of the joy. Johnathon was gone, and yet his child was on the way. The baby would be their one true link to the man who had meant so much to all of them. They all had to do their best to take care of Miranda as she went through this difficult time, and they would all need to be there when the baby was born, so that he or she could know the full circle of people who had been close to their father.

Astrid gently put down the photo. "I need to go. I have a headache. I'm so sorry." She kissed Miranda on the cheek, then Tara. "Thank you so much for a wonderful night. We should do this more often."

"That would be nice," Miranda said. "Can I show you out?"

"I can find my way. But thank you." Just like that, Astrid disappeared through the door.

"Do you think she's okay?" Miranda asked. "I hope that seeing the nursery didn't bother her."

"I think she's still processing Johnathon's death. Like all of us."

"So true." Miranda stepped over to the bookcase and adjusted the picture.

"Did Andrew say anything else while he was here?" Tara asked.

Miranda turned back and drew in a deep breath, seeming even more tired now than she had when they'd arrived. "He's a very conflicted man. I'm sure you know a lot about it, but he and Johnathon had a very rocky childhood and they didn't come out of it with a good relationship."

"Hard times bring some people together, but it can also tear them apart," Tara offered.

"Exactly," Miranda continued. "So, I don't know. He seemed to be going through the full range of emotions while he was here. He's definitely still harboring a lot of anger toward his brother. He said something about a botched deal. Which seems crazy to me. To my knowledge, Johnathon and Andrew were not working together on anything."

Tara was in the dark on that one. "I'm sorry you had to be on the receiving end of that."

"Yeah. I eventually just asked him to leave. I think that's why he sent the photo. I think he realized he'd gone a bit off the rails." Miranda paused for a moment and looked down at her feet. "Andrew and Johnathon are very alike. They both have the same temper. You must have experienced that at least once."

"Absolutely." Tara realized she might have been too quick to join in, but it was nice to be able to talk to someone who fully appreciated what it had been like to be married to a force of nature like Johnathon.

He'd been someone who felt things very intensely and expressed them as such.

"Although, to Johnathon's credit, the temper didn't appear very often. Most of the time, he was as loving as could be."

That hadn't quite been Tara's experience, but perhaps Johnathon had gotten better at being a husband the third time around. With Astrid gone, it felt as though it was Tara's time to leave, as well. "I should get out of your hair. I'm sure you'd love to get some sleep."

She nodded. "I would. Problem is that it's impossible to sleep in a house this big when you're here by yourself. It's almost too quiet. And I can't take a sleeping pill because of the baby."

Tara felt bad. This couldn't be great circumstances for dealing with her spouse's death. "Well, hopefully having dinner guests did something to wear you out a little."

Miranda flashed a smile. In that moment, Tara saw exactly what Johnathon must have loved about her—a warmth that radiated when she chose to share it. "I'll walk you downstairs."

"Sounds great." When they reached the front door, Tara turned to say her goodbye. "Thank you for tonight. And thank you for putting your trust in me. I hope that I can make our shares of Sterling even more valuable."

Miranda opened the door and leaned against the

edge of it. "I just need you to prove to me that this is a worthwhile venture."

"You mean a successful run at the Seaport Promenade?"

"I mean actually landing it. I know how the culture at Sterling works and if you fail at the outset, nobody will respect you. That's just the world Johnathon established. Win or go home."

Tara swallowed hard. She was starting to feel the pressure from all sides. "I'll do my best."

"And please. Talk to the city about naming something. I'd really love to see Johnathon's name memorialized for the entire city to see."

Once again, she found herself saying that she'd do her best.

Tara climbed into her car, but couldn't bring herself to start the engine. She stared off into space, thinking about everyone's competing wants and how she played a role in it. The whole process was so tiring. She slowly lowered her head until she could rest her forehead on the steering wheel. Why did she feel like she was holding the whole world together by a string? Maybe because she was.

Twelve

Win or go home. That was Tara's new mantra, and it had been for three weeks, ever since Miranda gave her a reality check about working at Sterling. It didn't matter that Tara had been at the company at the very beginning. It didn't matter that she personally had a stake. It only mattered that she produced results. She would get only one shot at making the Seaport project happen.

And so Tara had been working her butt off, and she was starting to see some payoff. Seaport was coming together in ways she'd never imagined. Yes, she'd had a vision, but Clay's experience, training and keen eye had brought in elements she never could've come up with on her own. Tara loved being around him and watching him work. He showed flashes of brilliance on a daily basis, which was helping them make up for the condensed timeline they had. The first presentations to the city would take place in a week and Clay's talent was the main reason they would be fully prepared.

Astrid had been quick to learn along the way and to soak up all the information she could. She had a knack for the small details, and for making sure everything ran smoothly, but Tara had witnessed tension between her and Clay. He'd try to be all business, but Tara saw the way he looked at her in unguarded moments—it was powerful. Frankly, it was a little hot. He'd then be detached and stern with Astrid, as if he was trying to create distance. For Astrid's part, she seemed oblivious to it, but at this point in her life, Tara figured that male attention must be something Astrid expected, rather than something that took her by surprise. Oddly enough, Tara found herself wanting to play matchmaker. After all, they were both physically stunning, divorced and unattached. Tara could see them together, even when she knew it was the stupidest idea ever. The Seaport project was too important, and romance always made things unnecessarily complicated. She'd learned that with Johnathon. And every day with Grant seemed to be another lesson in just how much business and pleasure did not mix.

It'd been three weeks since their big talk, the one where they'd decided they had to keep things professional and couldn't give in to their attraction. Since then, each day had been a new test. Tara found it nearly impossible to talk to him. He was still kind to her, but their rapport had gone cold. Gone was the flirting. There was no playful banter, none of the inside jokes, the sexy moments of eye contact or the occasional touch of his hand on her arm. Everything fun between them had evaporated into thin air and she would've been lying if she said there wasn't a part of her that desperately wanted it back.

Tara could've made peace with the all-business version of their relationship a little easier if Grant didn't continue to be so damn enticing. He'd let his five o'clock shadow fill in a bit. It wasn't quite a full-blown beard, but it did something to make Tara weak. It made the line of his jaw stronger and the dark hair really brought out his eyes. Leave it to Grant to find a way to make himself even more handsome. It wasn't fair.

It might not be so hard to deal with if she didn't have the memories of their one night together emblazoned in her memory. She found herself sitting in meetings with him, not concentrating on the important work of the Seaport project, and instead fixating on what his facial hair might feel like brushing against her cheek. Her lips. Any other part of her body he felt inclined to kiss. His presence made her squirm in her seat and be keenly aware of how one flash of his deep brown eyes was like an arrow into her chest. It was not an ideal way to get through the workday. She was spending a fair amount of time searching for air-conditioning vents to stand in front of. Grant had her running that hot.

Yes, she'd been the one to insist that they return to their previous platonic relationship. It was necessary for her to stay focused on business, the one place where she could finally build herself some true happiness and fulfillment. But it was feeling less and less possible. The workday was not enjoyable, even when they were making progress. It was pure stress, all because Grant did nothing to soften the hard edges. She never should have slept with him. She never should have let him get that close to her. She always did better when she kept men at arm's length. It was the up close and personal that always did her in.

Sandy rapped on Tara's office door. "Unless there's something else you need, I'm going to head out for the weekend," she said. It was Friday and Sandy was headed to Palm Springs for a getaway with her boyfriend.

"Can you bring me the Seaport binder? I'd like to go over it one more time before I head out."

Pure concern crossed Sandy's face. "I've been over every detail at least fifty times, Ms. Sterling. Clay will have the final renderings ready on Monday. I'll pull together the presentation on Tuesday, you and Clay can rehearse it on Wednesday and Thursday, and you'll be ready to go next Friday."

Tara appreciated that Sandy was an excellent assistant, and it was her job to take care of the minute details that Tara shouldn't have to worry about. It still didn't make her any less worried about the things that might go wrong. That had been the advantage of working on her own for all those years as a real estate agent. She got to watch over every point herself. "I just want to give it one more look while we still have time to make changes."

"Sure. Of course." Sandy returned several minutes later with the binder, which she placed on Tara's desk. "Oh, and I just forwarded that status report on the other project sites you asked me to research."

Tara had given Sandy a list of parcels of land available for purchase in and around the county and asked her to compile information like listing price, acreage, site limitations and advantages. "Already?"

Sandy smiled. "I figured you wanted it as soon as possible."

Tara pulled up the email on her laptop, eager to see what Sandy had come up with. Tara wanted Grant to know that the Seaport project wasn't the end and beginning of her aspirations at Sterling. "I do. Thank you for getting to that so quickly. You're amazing."

"Just doing my job."

"Well, thank you. Have a great weekend."

"You too, Ms. Sterling."

Sandy left and Tara got to work, reading over the report and making notes to herself of which sites had the biggest upside, in order to narrow her choices. She wanted to go to Grant with the best possible project, one that would bowl him over and hopefully convince him that she had what it took to be great at her job. She glanced at the clock on her computer when she was finished. It was already nearly six. She got up out of her seat to stretch, knowing it was time for her to call it a day and head home. She should be out on her balcony right now, gazing at the ocean and drinking a glass of wine. The only trouble was there wasn't anything or anyone waiting for her at home. Just like there hadn't been in so long.

"One more thing," she muttered to herself, plopping back down in her seat and opening up the binder for the Seaport project. She carefully scanned the pages of their draft proposal, getting more excited about presenting it to the city next week. Yes, she was biased, but she was proud of the work they'd done. It was innovative and smart. Surely it would be a slam dunk for them to pass this first round and move on to the finals where the sizable field of developers would be whittled down to three. Then they would take feedback from the city, make revisions and submit a final plan.

She was just about to close the binder when something caught her eye—a detail so essential it would have been impossible to miss—the orientation of the buildings on the site. It could be windy down by the water, and the city had been specific with what they wanted.

Tara could've sworn that the original spec information had said they wanted buildings facing to the northwest. But this said southwest. She flipped back and forth, between the pages from the city and the small-scale renderings Clay had done—all of which faced the northwest, the wrong direction.

Tara shot up out of her seat, grabbed her phone and marched down the hall. She'd worried that something could go wrong with this project at any moment. She just hadn't expected it would be now. Six fifteen in the evening on a Friday, with only a week until presentation day. The office was eerily quiet. Almost everyone had gone home. She wound her way around to Clay's office, hoping this was all a mistake. Maybe the drawings in the binder were old. Except that didn't make sense at all. Everything had always been to the northwest. Her original concept had been that way. Was this all her fault?

She knocked on Clay's door, but there was no answer. She rattled the doorknob and it was locked. Her heart was pounding, her pulse racing so fast it made it hard to think. But she had to do exactly that. *Sandy.* She pulled up her assistant's number, but it only rang once before going to voice mail. "Dammit." Tara looked to her right and then to her left. The light was still on in Grant's office. He was her only hope.

She drew in a deep breath and steeled herself for his reaction. She had wanted so badly for this project to go perfectly. She had wanted Grant to see her as fully capable, not just the woman who'd had a sizable chunk of a company land in her lap. This would have been an easier conversation a month ago, when she and Grant were still enjoying the warmth of their friendship. But everything had gone cold, all because of sex.

Tara barged into Grant's office like a tornado in heels. "We have a problem."

Yes, we do. Grant nearly uttered the words out loud, but he knew better. He was having little luck getting used to the idea of them being nothing more than colleagues. It had been three weeks of that exercise, and Grant felt as though he was experiencing the slowest, most painful death possible. It killed him to be around her. It killed him to keep her at a distance, but that was what was required. "I was just about to head home. Maybe we can talk about this on Monday?" He shuffled papers on his desk so that he wouldn't have to look at her. He'd damn near perfected the art of avoiding the vision of her. In meetings where she was present, he'd stare at documents, and when she dropped by his office, he typically resorted to directing his attention to his computer. Anything to avoid looking at what he couldn't have.

Tara dropped a large binder on his desk with a thud. Grant jumped. He couldn't help it. It wasn't like her to be so forceful. The cover of the folder said Seaport Promenade. "Grant. I'm serious. We have a crisis. And I need you to look at me. We need to talk. Now."

He begrudgingly did as she asked, his sights traveling from her hands and up her toned arms, to her sculpted shoulders, graceful neck and ultimately to that face. The one he had no answer for. He didn't know why looking at her made him feel so powerless, but it did. Her lips were ridiculously kissable right now, even when the corners were turned down with an expression that spoke of nothing but being unhappy. "Yeah. Okay. You have my full and undivided attention." *Even if it kills me.*

"I made a mistake with the Seaport project. A big one."

"So fix it. You still have a week. This stuff happens all the time. It's always a fire drill when you're at the finish line."

She shook her head slowly from side to side, as if she could tell him how deeply serious this was by sending wafts of her perfume his way. If only she knew how distracting it was. "You don't understand. I misread the site orientation. Our entire plan needs a ninety-degree turn."

Grant then realized why she was so deadly serious. This was indeed a major gaffe. "You can't do that. You'll have to rethink the entire project." His mind went to elevations and utilities. The placement of exterior doors and the flow of people. "There's no way there's enough time to get it done. Clay's gone for the weekend and I can't call him in. He took his daughter up to Anaheim to do the theme parks for her birthday. I promised I wouldn't even send him a text." Maybe this was for the best. If Grant couldn't have Tara, he might as well keep control of Sterling. Astrid and Miranda would likely recant their support of Tara's idea when they found out about her error and that it might cost them the project.

Tara slumped into one of the chairs in front of his desk. "I messed up. Big time." There was a small quiver in her voice, one that was rarely there. In fact, Grant hadn't heard it since the day of Johnathon's accident.

"I don't understand what happened."

"I don't either. I swear I went over the city's requirements a million times. So did Sandy. There must have been a miscommunication along the line somewhere."

Grant didn't want to tell Tara that he'd warned her that working with the city could be a very big pain, even when her problem was solid evidence of that very fact. "Maybe this wasn't meant to be, Tara. I'm sorry."

"I can't just give up. I've put so much work into this. So has Astrid. And Clay. We have to at least try to save it."

"Sometimes we put a lot of effort into something and it doesn't work out." This was an apt description of his situation with Tara. He'd tried to let her know that he wanted more, but at every turn, she was trying to push him away.

"Don't treat me like a first grader. This isn't a school project. This is millions of dollars. This is me proving my worth." Again, her voice wobbled, but this time the falter was much more dramatic. She got up out of the chair, seeking the refuge of the window, where she could turn away from him. Where she could hide. Again.

"Hey. It's okay to be upset. I won't hold it against you if you cry."

"I am *not* going to cry." There was a determined sob hiding behind the word *not*.

"You don't have to be so tough all the time. It's okay to allow yourself a human moment, even when we're talking about work."

"You don't understand." She sniffled. "This is me basically proving Johnathon's theory about why I shouldn't be here. He was convinced I would make a big mistake and it would be impossible for him to reprimand me because of our marriage. Now you're being soft on me because of our friendship. Well, what's left of it."

"Don't say that." Grant got up from his seat and approached her slowly. This was so much like their meeting a few weeks ago, it felt like a déjà vu. Once again, she was doing everything to keep him at arm's length, even when there was some small part of her that was willing to admit that she needed him and his help. "What can I do?"

Tara shot him a look over her shoulder, then turned her sights to the floor as she began pacing. "You know you don't want to do anything. You were against this project from the very beginning. You're probably happy it's turned out this way. It's a prime example of you being the person who should be in charge and me being the person who's running to try to catch up with you."

Yes, it was absolutely against his best business interests to help Tara. If he was smart, he'd leave her to deal with her own mess and he'd quietly claim victory. But he didn't have it in him. There was this voice in the back of his head that knew two things—he could not be like Johnathon and push her aside, and he could not ignore the feelings he had for her, even when he'd lied and said he was fine with them being nothing more than colleagues. "Don't talk about yourself that way. None of that is true. Even though you have a lot of experience in this world, you're still learning. It's okay to make mistakes."

She shot him a pitiful look that stopped him dead in his tracks. This blunder might take down tough-as-nails Tara. "This is the dumbest mistake ever. Only an idiot would make it."

It didn't make sense that someone as thorough as Tara would make a flub like this, but perhaps she'd let her enthusiasm get the best of her. "I've made far worse."

"Name one."

Carrying a torch for her came to mind, but once again, he kept his thoughts to himself. "Look. Do you want my help or not? Because if you don't, I'm going home for the weekend." He walked back behind his desk and powered down his computer. Silence seemed to swell in the confined space of his office. He could easily imagine her saying no. She likely already regretted that she'd allowed herself such a moment of weakness.

"No. I do want your help." She took a step toward his desk. "If you truly want to help me, that is. I would understand if you just let me deal with this on my own."

He drew in a deep breath through his nose and mustered the courage to look at her. The sun through the window was showing off every inch of her delicious curves in silhouette. It made his hands twitch to think about touching her. He wanted to do it so badly. "Your mistake is Sterling's mistake. And the reality is that a lot of our competitors are in this hunt. They all know we're in it, so saving face is a worthwhile investment. We can't show up at the presentation with the wrong orientation. We'll look incompetent, and I certainly don't want that."

"If you're trying to cheer me up, it isn't working."

He laughed quietly. "I'm saying that I do have a reason to help you. And more than anything, I don't want to see you fail." There was only one solution to this and it was staring him in the face. He was duly torn by what he saw as a logical answer—part of him wanted to have so much time with her. And another part of him knew how much it hurt when she tore herself away. "With Clay out of town, you and I are the only ones who can fix this. Which means we're going to have to work all weekend."

"How can we possibly do it without an architect?"

"I don't do renderings and site plans anymore, but I am still licensed. We can at least come up with a workable plan to bring to Clay on Monday morning. We'll just have to hope that he can pull it off by next Friday."

"You'd do that for me?"

In an instant, he wanted to say. "I'd do it for the firm. As I said, I don't want us to look bad in front of our competitors. I'd rather squash them like a bug."

"This means so much to me. Truly. It means the world that you'd want to help. How do you want to do this? Should we set up a space in one of the conference rooms?"

Grant then saw that this might be a glimmer of what he thought he might not get again—one more chance with Tara. "No. We'll work at my house. All weekend." He was pleased with the fact that he'd come out with it with so much confidence. That wasn't what he was feeling, at all. Still, he knew that this might be his final opportunity with her. He stood a much greater chance of showing her that they could work together in more ways than one while they were at his place. And he was far more likely to finally come clean with the things he'd been hiding for a decade if he'd at least had a glass of wine or two.

"The two of us? Alone? Are you sure that's a good idea?"

"It was different a month ago. The office atmosphere was still shaky after Johnathon's death. I think we've all started to come to terms with it."

"Okay then." She nodded eagerly as she took the binder from his desk. "I'll run home and change before I come over."

"And pack a bag, Tara. I have a feeling you're going to want to stay over."

Thirteen

Despite having designs on Tara, Grant refused to be obvious in setting the stage for romance. He couldn't handle any more rejection from her. No, if he was going to have the chance to kiss her again, and perhaps take her to bed, he needed it to happen of its own accord. He might give it a nudge here or there, but it would ultimately be something that happened between them because they both wanted it wholeheartedly. No more reservations. No more second-guessing whether it was a good idea.

He knew what a dangerous line he was walking. Tara and the other wives still held all of the cards when it came to Sterling. If they wanted him out, they could make it happen. But here he had a chance to play a role in the Seaport proposal. At worst, he could make the case that he'd done everything to save Tara's pet project. That had to earn him at least a few brownie points with the wives.

Grant had set up a work area at the table in his informal dining area next to the kitchen. He opened one of the sliding glass doors to let in the ocean breeze. This was one of the most spectacular views on his property—tall frameless windows showed off the windblown landscape of his backyard—palm trees and a seemingly endless stretch of bright green grass, which dropped off to the Pacific below.

He'd stood out near the edge of that cliff many times and thought about Tara, across the bay in Coronado. He'd done it when he had women with him. He'd done it when he had women in his bed, waiting for him to return. Perhaps it was just that Tara had always felt like unfinished business. They had an unbelievable connection, and for so long, Johnathon had been in the way. Now that was no longer true, and he really didn't want the business of Sterling Enterprises to be the roadblock anymore. If he and Tara were not meant to be, he could accept that, but only if it was because she couldn't return his feelings. He was tired of letting other factors stand between him and a glimmer of happiness.

Tara arrived a little after eight o'clock, looking absolutely breathtaking in a pair of jeans and a turquoise top that clung to every curve. It was a nice and casual counterpoint to her usual businesslike demeanor. "I'm freaking out," she said, breezing past him.

He closed the door and followed her through the foyer, down the central corridor to the back of the house where the kitchen and great room were. "Don't panic. All we can do is try."

"I appreciate that, but I'm still panicked. Miranda and Astrid are going to wonder what in the world I'm doing."

"That's between you three." Once again, he wasn't about to let anyone else stand between Tara and him. "For now, I think that saving yourself and your pet project is the right call. Plus, Clay has sunk a ton of hours into this already. We can't let all of that go to waste."

She sighed and shook her head. "Do you have any wine?"

Grant was so relieved he hadn't had to offer. "Of course."

Tara took a seat at the kitchen island while he pulled out a bottle from the fridge. "White okay?"

"Yes. Red gives me a headache sometimes."

"We don't want that."

"Not tonight, that's for sure." She smoothed her hand over the white marble countertops, looking all over the room. "I forgot how incredible your house is. I haven't been here in so long. Eight years, maybe?"

"Sounds about right. I don't think you've been here since you and Johnathon got divorced." He offered her a glass. "I'd like to propose a toast. To fixing mistakes."

She smiled and clinked her glass with his. "It's really sweet of you to do this."

"Please don't start with the nice-guy routine." He rounded the kitchen island so he could stand next to her.

"Oh, I won't. The guy who wants to squash the competition like a bug is definitely not a good guy."

He and Tara sat at the table and got right to work. She went over the site limitations, the city's requirements and the plan as it was. She and Clay had made quite a lot of changes since Grant had last been in the loop several weeks ago. Even though she was in a trouble spot with the deadline looming, once she started talking her way through it, he could see exactly how capable she was of doing this job. Hell, she could run Sterling if she truly wanted to do that. It made Grant sad to think that might end up being the case, and he would fight for his rightful place at the company, but if he had to lose to someone, Tara would be a hell of a victor.

After an hour or so of discussion of possible changes, Grant took out a large pad of drafting paper and began working on a rough sketch of the new layout. It would ultimately take far more detail than what he was able to create here. For now, he and Tara were concerned with the flow of pedestrians and bicycle traffic, along with ample handicapped accessibility. There were noise issues to think about with the live music venue they were proposing, and then there were the aesthetics—the way it would look from both the water and the city sides of the project. In truth, it was a mountain of work, and Grant was truly burned out by one in the morning.

"I don't know if I can work anymore tonight," he said, leaning back in his chair and stretching his arms high above his head.

Tara finished off her glass of wine. "Do you think this is feasible?" She tapped the stack of sketches he'd done so far. They were incredibly rough and would take some explaining to Clay, but they were a solid start.

"I do. I mean, you and I need to figure out the elevations since some of the structures have had to be moved out of the previous order. But we have to-morrow. And Sunday."

It was Tara's turn to sit back in her chair and stretch, showing off the lithe lines of her beautiful body. Everything in Grant's body went tight. Even under the strain of sheer exhaustion, he wanted her.

"You and I make a good team. I'm sorry that this project had to be so adversarial," she said.

Grant shrugged and sat forward, drawing a circle with his finger on the pad of paper before him. He wanted so badly to touch her. To kiss her. To take her to bed. "I'm the one who should be saying I'm sorry. I knew from the night of the baseball game that you had an incredible vision. And I should've stayed fully on board with that. I should've backed you up, rather than letting you sink or swim."

"You were protecting your position within Sterling. As the person carving out her own spot in that company, I have to admire that."

She was being gracious and Grant was exceptionally tired of the obstacles they'd faced. He really wanted to strip it all away until there was nothing left but the two of them. "It's not more important than our friendship."

"Do you mean that? Because there are times when I doubted that."

"Our friendship? When?"

"The last few weeks. You were so cold to me in the office. I felt like I'd been demoted or something. It was so clear that you'd drawn the battle lines and saw our relationship as combative."

He shook his head and sat back farther in his chair, stuffing his hands into his pockets. "I only felt that way because we went from sharing the most amazing night ever to you being too worried about what Astrid and Miranda might think."

"You were equally worried about office gossip."

"And that died back pretty quickly. Which means my attitude toward you at work did its job."

"I still didn't like it."

Grant swallowed back the emotion of the moment. "I didn't like it either. I hated every minute of it. I don't like being cool to you, Tara."

Tara bit down on her lower lip like she was fighting a smile. "Our night together was pretty amazing, wasn't it?"

"The absolute best." He answered a little too quickly, but it was exactly the way he felt. "And I'm not exaggerating."

"But the business is standing between us."

"Only if we let it."

She eyed him with suspicion, scanning his face like she was looking for clues. Did she not trust him? Was she truly more loyal to the wives than she was to him? Or would it all come down to being nothing more than business? "You don't really mean that," she said.

Grant pushed aside the papers and stood. He easily took the two short strides to Tara's side, but it felt as though he was crossing a dividing line. He placed his hand on her upper arm and walked behind her, not letting go as he used his other hand to pull her hair back from her shoulder. All the while, ocean breezes streamed in through the open slider door, heightening every sense—touch, smell and sight. He lowered his head and spoke into her ear. "I've never been more serious about anything in my entire life."

With his breath hot against the nape of her neck, Grant was taking charge again. And Tara was completely powerless against it. She wanted him just as much as she'd wanted him before. Possibly more. The last several weeks of fighting back her attraction to him had been pure hell. He'd been cold to her and she wanted him warm again. She wanted his white-hot body against hers.

She turned her head to make eye contact, to be sure that he wanted what she did, but he countered not with his gaze, but with his mouth on hers and his hand at her nape. He pulled her head back to deepen the kiss, their tongues quickly finding the satisfying dance they'd discovered mere weeks ago. Tara's entire body flooded with heat and desire. Craving. Unlike before, this wasn't about curiosity, this was about another taste of this man she couldn't get out of her system.

She stood to be closer to him and he walked her back to the kitchen island, pressing her backside against the counter. She grabbed him by the waist and tugged him closer, wanting him to flatten her right then and there. He was hard already; she could feel it through his jeans, and it made anticipation bubble up inside her.

Tara lifted one butt cheek and eased herself up onto the countertop, wrapping her legs around Grant and muscling him close. His erection rubbed right against her center, and even through several layers of denim, it made her so hot. He kissed her deeply, their noses bumping into each other, and she placed her hands on either side of his face, rubbing her thumbs against the thicker texture of his facial hair. It was somewhere between silky and scratchy, and she loved the contrast in sensations. It so perfectly mirrored her inner conflict about making love with him again. She knew she shouldn't, that sex would only make things more complicated, but she also knew that she was tired of waiting for happiness, and if this was the only blip of it she got for the foreseeable future, she'd better grab it while she could.

She pulled at the lightweight sweater Grant wore, tugging it up over his head. She spread her hands across his chest, kissing his warm skin. His muscles seemed to twitch beneath her touch, and she loved having that effect on him. "You are too sexy, Grant. Working with you while staying away from you is impossible." That was an issue she was going to have to resolve, but not now. Not when she had a one-way ticket to his bedroom and they had an entire weekend stretching out before them. Astrid wouldn't find her here. Not this time. They could be all alone.

Grant growled into her ear. "You have no idea how much I love hearing that."

Before she could respond, he'd lifted her off the kitchen island and was walking her to the back of the house. Tara was a tall woman—she'd never been whisked off to bed like this, and she loved the way it made her feel so desired. She spent so much of her day trying to be tough and formidable. It was wonderful to feel as though she was at someone else's mercy.

When they arrived at Grant's bedroom, he didn't bother with the light, but instead laid her down on the bed and put all of his body weight on hers. The kiss they fell into had no limits—she could have kissed him forever and she would have made time for more. She didn't want it to end. She also wanted him to know that she was his equal partner in this endeavor, so she rolled to her side, taking him with her. He eased to his back and she straddled his hips, grinding her center against him as she sat up, crossed her arms at the waist and lifted her top up over her head. She wanted Grant's hands all over her, but he instead folded his arms back behind his head.

"Don't you want to take my bra off?" she asked.

"I like watching you do it," he answered playfully.

"Fair enough." He'd made the first move. He deserved to have his way at least a little bit. She reached behind her and unhooked the garment, then teased one strap from her shoulder, then the other, before she flung it aside. His hands found her breasts, and molded around them, teasing her nipples and causing her breath to hitch. His touch was pure magic, his hands warm and purely focused on her pleasure. It felt so good that she gasped, and she dropped her head back, letting her hair cascade down her naked shoulders. Grant took his chance to unbutton and unzip her jeans and Tara realized just how impatient she was for the main event. She wanted Grant naked and she wanted the same for herself.

She hopped off the bed and quickly shucked her jeans, while Grant followed her lead, climbing off the mattress and leaving his pants on the floor. He pulled back the silky duvet and picked her up again, this time sweeping her legs up with his arm. He planted a knee on the bed and placed her gently against the cool sheets. She swished her hand against the smooth fabric, but arched her back. The need for him to be touching her and weighing her down again was too much.

He reached into his bedside drawer and pulled out a condom, which he rolled on himself. She waited in anticipation as he climbed into bed and kissed her again, but this time there was something about it that truly made her breath catch. It was so intense it felt like he was sending a message. Perhaps he was trying to say he was sorry for the cold shoulder all of these weeks. Sorry for the many arguments they'd had.

He put his arms around her and urged her on top of him. Tara eagerly accepted the challenge, rising up onto her knees, and then taking his length in her hand. She guided him inside and sank down against his body, soaking up every blissful second of the way he filled her so perfectly. They began to move together and he took his time with the rotation of his hips, hitting her center in just the right spot, already pushing her close to the edge. She struggled to stay in the moment and not let her mind wander. The pure ecstasy made it a difficult proposition. He felt too good inside her, and she slipped into a daydream about what it would be like to actually be with a man who was her match. Was Grant that man? Could they work past all that stood between them?

She struggled for her breaths as the pressure

began to build. She kissed him and caught just how shallow his own breath had become. It was clear that they were both close, and she was torn between wanting to cross the goal line and wanting it to last forever. This right now was perfect. As messy as everything around them could be, being in bed with Grant at this moment was where she belonged. No question about that. The orgasm barreled into her from out of nowhere, shattering the tension between them. Grant followed almost immediately and they were both calling out, a chorus of pleasured and breathless words.

She collapsed at his side and spread her hand across his chest as he wrapped his arm around her. He smoothed her hair back, and kissed the top of her head. Over and over again. Each kiss came with a tiny tug, bringing her closer to him. Contentment blanketed her body just as his body heat poured into her. She couldn't remember feeling like this with a man before. Not with anyone who'd come before him. She and Grant were equals. They were friends. And they would always have a connection. Now deeper than the one they'd had before.

Fourteen

Tara slept over for two nights. There wasn't much sleeping going on, but that was better than fine with Grant. He wanted this to go on forever—Tara in his bed, giving him untold pleasures and welcoming his touch. They'd quickly reached the point where he could simply walk up to her, take her in his arms and kiss her. He didn't want to call it a fantasy brought to life. It was more like a dream, and it felt like that, seeing her walk around his home in bare feet, watching her wrap her hair up in a towel after a shower, bearing witness to the moment when she woke up in his bed. She was what this house had been missing. She was the missing puzzle piece in his life.

He had to find a way to tell her before she had the chance to go home. It was Sunday morning and they'd already made love twice and had breakfast. They'd long since finished as much of the Seaport proposal as they could without Clay's help. It was only a matter of time before she'd be gone, they'd return to their previous arrangement at Sterling and he'd be in the hot seat. If she was successful with the Seaport pitch, he might lose his hold on the company. He was essentially standing in her way, and he already knew that her relationship with Astrid and Miranda had grown stronger.

But there was another way out of this, at least as far as Grant saw it. They could run the company together, as a true partnership, in the office and out. Could Tara ever see them that way or had this been just another instance of him being lucky enough to get her into bed? Would she ever want to share that lead role at work? Or would strong and determined Tara, the woman dead set on winning at all costs, simply decide that Grant didn't measure up? Would she ultimately reach the conclusion that she was too much for him?

"This weekend has been amazing." Grant put the last plate from breakfast in the dishwasher.

Tara was seated at the kitchen island, still hugging her mug of coffee in her hands. She turned her sights to the backyard and the Pacific. The palm trees rustled in the wind, the sun casting short shadows on the grass. He studied her profile, and it was hard not to see her through the lens of everything she'd been through. She'd had so much loss in her life, and still she kept forging ahead. She was a survivor and that was not only what he adored in her, but it was the quality he feared most. Could she ever need him the way he needed her?

"It really was." She took a sip of her coffee and turned to look at him. "Thank you so much for saving my butt with the Seaport project. It remains to be seen whether or not Clay and I can actually pull this off, but I couldn't have put us in that position without your help. So thank you."

Grant walked around to her side of the island and stood next to her. "I think we make a great team." He believed that in every sense, and he wanted to tell her as much. *I love you. I have always loved you.* The words were swimming around in his head, but he couldn't begin to imagine he would ever have the perfect chance to utter them, to say them in a way that wouldn't scare her off and send her running.

"About that. I know you've been against this project from the beginning, but would you consider coming with me to the presentation on Friday? We could use a heavy hitter like you."

Grant wanted to be supportive, but he also wanted to give Tara the chance to shine. He hadn't been in on this project from the ground floor and plenty of people in the office knew he had reservations about it. If he was going to convince her that they should run Sterling together, she would need her own win to show the staff that she was there because she'd earned it. He didn't want to put her in the position

Johnathon had all those years ago, of being marginalized because she happened to be romantically entangled with the CEO.

"I don't think you need my help. I really don't."

Tara frowned and peered up at him with those big blue eyes that somehow seemed to reflect the whole world. "After all of the work we did? You don't want to take credit? I thought you wanted to step out from behind the shadow of Johnathon. I thought it was time for you to put your career first."

"Maybe I'm tired of doing that. Maybe I want you to have your own win, Tara."

"Or maybe you're trying to save your own hide because you don't truly believe in this project."

He had to be honest. "I'm still not sold on Seaport. I'm sorry. I wish I was. But I am sold on you and your vision. If anyone can make this work, it's you."

Tara shook her head and got up from her seat, the barstool leg scraping against the floor. "I was worried about this. You don't want to put your name on this project. You don't want to put your stamp of approval on it."

He reached for her, over what felt like a monumental difference. "I told you. I want you to have your own win."

She scanned his face as if she was looking for answers or perhaps some hint that he wasn't being truthful. He wasn't sure what he had to do to convince her. "I know you, Grant. You'll always put your career first. That's why you never got married. That's why you could never settle on one woman."

He almost wanted to laugh at that. The assumption she'd made was remarkably off base. "That's not the reason."

"Johnathon always said you were the perfect partner because you were married to your work."

Grant didn't want to get angry with the dead. He'd already done plenty of that as far as Johnathon was concerned. But he greatly disliked that his best friend had painted him in that light. It couldn't have been further from the truth. "I worked hard. That much is true. But that was because I believed in the vision of the company and I enjoyed the challenges I had set out before me. But it's not the reason I never got married."

She smirked and cocked an eyebrow at him. "Right. Too many fish in the sea."

He shook his head. "No. I never settled down because I couldn't have the perfect woman."

"You mean you couldn't *find* the perfect woman. That's a myth, by the way. There is no perfect person."

But there was. At least for him.

"Look, Tara. This weekend has shown me a lot. You and I work well together in every sense. But I have feelings for you. Strong feelings." That was as far out on the ledge as he could go. He was still gunshy. Her rejection stung that badly.

Tara swallowed hard. "How am I supposed to believe that when just last week you were being truly unkind to me? How am I supposed to believe that when you won't stand by my side and make the presentation with me?"

"You have to believe it because it's true. I know that you said you only want to see me as a colleague, but I need you to at least try to see me as more than that. And if you don't, I think we're at an impasse. I can't work with you and feel the way I feel about you. I couldn't do it when Sterling was first getting started and I can't do it now." As soon as he'd said the words, he realized that he'd finally let the cat out of the bag.

"What did you say?" There was already an edge of betrayal in her voice, like she knew what was coming.

"I don't want to dredge up the past. I want to talk about the here and now. About us. About everything that happened this weekend. It has meant something to me. I think I'm falling in love with you." The words had been tumbling around in his head for so long that it was liberating to finally say them. It was also scary as hell.

"No. Don't muddy the waters by saying that to me. I want you to tell me what you were talking about when you said that you couldn't work with me when Sterling was first getting started."

It was time to finally come clean, even when he knew this might be the point of no return. She might never forgive him for what he was about to say. "When Johnathon told me his concerns about having you work at the company, I sided with him. I told him that it was better if you went."

Tara's jaw tightened and her eyes blazed with a hurt he'd never seen. "Excuse me? You bought into that whole idea that we couldn't work together because we were married?" She shook her head and crossed her arms, as if she needed to protect herself from him. "I can't believe you backed him up on that. It was the stupidest excuse ever."

He sucked in a deep breath to steel himself, hoping against hope that he could make a plausible argument for why what he'd done before was wrong, but he was prepared to make amends now. "That wasn't the argument he made, Tara. He may have told you that, but that wasn't what he said to me."

Tara's eyes were wide and pleading. "Then what did he say?"

"He called you a distraction."

"We were married. I was nothing of the sort. If I was, he wouldn't have left me."

Once again, Grant was tempted to curse Johnathon. She wasn't wrong. As soon as she'd been out of the company, Johnathon's eyes began to wander. He knew that had hurt her, but those weren't his wounds to heal. He had to focus on the things he'd done and the reasons for his actions. "You were a distraction for *me*. He saw the way I looked at you. He knew that I never got past that first night when we met. I tried, Tara, but it was impossible. I think it would have been different if you hadn't ended up with Johnathon."

"So this was all about you two trying to outdo each other? He had to win and you just couldn't stand the fact that he had?"

He reached for her, but she pulled away. It felt as though his heart was being torn from his chest as he once again relived the history he had with Johnathon and Tara. All of the nights when they'd gone out, all of the dinners at each other's houses. The vacations, where he'd drag along whatever woman he was seeing at the time, but really only wanted Tara. He felt such shame over that, but it was the truth. Grant had to watch his best friend be with the woman he wanted and there was nothing he could do about it. "No. It was about seeing how amazing you were, and experiencing our connection, but not being able to act on it. It drove me crazy."

"I have to go." She stalked down the hall back to the bedroom.

Grant thought for a moment about just letting her go, but he knew that it would be forever. And he couldn't live with that. He was so tired of living with regret. So he followed her. When he arrived in his room, she was stuffing her clothes into her overnight bag. "Can we please talk about this? I feel like this has gone sideways."

"I need space to think, Grant." She planted one hand on her hip and the other at her forehead. She stared off into space, her eyes darting from side to side. "I find it very hard to believe that you were carrying a torch for me all these years, Grant. You had no problem distracting yourself, and it's not like you didn't have plenty of opportunity after Johnathon ended our marriage."

"But..." he started.

She turned on him. "No. I think this is about you and Johnathon. He thought of me as a prize to snatch away from you, and you never forgave him for it. I think you felt that same way about Sterling, and then he went and died, but he screwed you over when he gave the wives the shares of the company. So now you have a new thing you can't forgive him for and that's made you decide that I'm the thing to be won."

He reached for her arm and her vision flew to his hand. It made him drop his grip. "Do you want to know what I think? I think you're afraid to let anyone in. Johnathon destroyed you when he left you and you never recovered. And then you lost your dad, so you built up this wall and convinced yourself that the best way to never lose again was to never get involved. To never get close to anyone again. I just want you to let down your guard and let me in. That's all I want."

She pressed her lips together tightly, fighting back tears. "You think you have me figured out, Grant, but you don't. I let plenty of people in. I'm just choosy when I do it. And I don't think I can choose you."

"Why?"

"We have too many competing wants. It's what

destroyed my marriage with Johnathon and it would only destroy us."

"Are you saying you don't have feelings for me, too? Because if that's the case, I swear I'll never bring it up again."

"I think my problem is I have too many feelings for you right now, Grant. And not all of them are good ones."

Fifteen

Tara arrived at work on the day of the big presentation with a headache the size of San Diego County. She'd been working like crazy all week, but so had Clay and Astrid. The three of them were all going the extra mile to make this happen, which was a bigger workload than expected. Sandy had called in sick every day this week. Apparently she'd picked up a bug of some sort in Palm Springs.

There had been many times when Tara had considered soliciting Grant's help, but he'd been keeping his distance. She felt bad about the argument they'd had at his house, and she wanted to apologize for her role in it, but she had to get through the presentation. It was a huge hurdle, one she'd been staring down for weeks, and deep down, she knew that the outcome would determine her course from here on out. If it went well, she'd try to stay at Sterling, and hope to find a working arrangement with Grant. If it went badly, she'd leave. It was the only logical answer. She'd sell off her shares to Grant or possibly just give them to him. He'd more than earned them.

As for the personal side of their relationship, that was an entirely different conversation. She was still wrapping her head around the things he'd said on Sunday, especially the part about her unwillingness to let people get close to her. She couldn't help it—distance had become her default. It made things easier. It made it possible to survive. There'd been so much hurt and loss in her life, but she'd always found a way to forge ahead. She couldn't allow herself to be wounded. But perhaps her persistence had been her downfall. She hadn't taken the time to slow down and see what was around her. Perhaps it was a case of trying to be a moving target—it made her harder to hit.

As for what this realization meant for the question of love, she wasn't sure. She cared about Grant deeply. She was closer to him than any person she knew. He'd become her best friend, and at times, her biggest champion. But they'd spent so much time in opposition to each other that it was hard to figure out what the good times had meant. Were they an aberration? A break from the contention around the office? Or had he truly fallen for her? Did he really want more? She knew she wanted more, but she also needed more—a guarantee of some sort. A sign that if she let Grant in, that he'd stay. That if he truly loved her, he'd love her forever. She couldn't take another loss, and losing her friendship with Grant would be a crushing blow.

Astrid knocked on Tara's office door, then waved a piece of paper in the air. "I don't think Sandy was sick all week."

"Why do you say that?"

"Read this." Astrid set the fax on Tara's desk. It was a resignation letter, with no explanation from Sandy, other than the fact that she was quitting. It was such a shame—she'd been an integral part of the team.

"Did I do something wrong?" If this was an omen of how things were going to go today, Tara was wondering if it might be time to throw in the towel.

Astrid shook her head. "I doubt it. She probably took a job somewhere else."

"Maybe." None of this sat well with Tara, but she needed to focus on the task ahead. Then she could begin the process of finding her way with Grant. "Let's finish getting packed up, grab Clay and head over."

It took about a half hour to load the model and presentation boards into a Sterling Enterprises van. The three rode over with Clay driving, to a large meeting space the city had rented in one of the hotels near the Seaport location. There was a bustle of activity when they arrived. It was hard not to ogle the models from the other firms that would be presenting. It was hard not to feel intimidated by the whole thing. There were a lot of heavy hitters filing inside, people who Tara had read about or Johnathon had pointed out at social functions. Many were CEO or president of their company. It only underscored Grant's lack of confidence in the project. He hadn't changed his mind about joining her today. If he had, he would have said something.

They went inside and set up their materials as instructed, then waited for their turn to make their case. The competing firms were not allowed in the room as one team was presenting, which left Tara to pace in the hall.

"Please stop," Astrid said with a hand on Tara's arm. "It will be fine."

Clay cast a doubtful look at them both. "You don't know that. It might not be fine."

Astrid returned his unpleasant expression. "Don't be so negative. All we can do is try."

Tara stopped her pacing, but that left her to lean against the wall and tap her foot. Damn, she wished Grant was here. She wished he believed in the things she did. She wished they could find a way, together.

A few minutes later, the Sterling team was called into the room. As Tara crossed the threshold and saw the long table of representatives from the city waiting to be dazzled, she had absolutely every reason to be intimidated. This was it. Do or die.

"Ladies and gentlemen, my name is Tara Sterling

and I'm here to represent Sterling Enterprises. We're very excited for the opportunity to present our plan for the Seaport Promenade."

Miraculously, it all clicked into place—she and Clay made an amazing team, playing off each other, and explaining the vision that Tara had originally had, fixed by Grant after Tara had made her big mistake, and finally brought to life by Clay's brilliance. When they were done and exited the room, Astrid and the normally subdued Clay were both ecstatic.

"Okay. I was wrong. That went well," Clay said.

"I told you." Astrid swatted his arm. "Now we wait for the city's answer on Monday."

Tara had to force her smile. It *had* gone incredibly well. But it felt empty. It wasn't the same without Grant here. It didn't feel like the win she was supposed to get. Not even close. It felt like it meant nothing, all because Grant hadn't been there to witness it. The thought made her incredibly sad, but it also made her realize that the biggest mistake she'd made wasn't on the plans for the Seaport site. It had been in letting work, once again, determine her course. She should have worked everything out with Grant first—the personal stuff—and she'd waited an entire week. Once again, she'd let distance be her buffer.

"Let's head back," Tara said. "I want to give Grant a full report." Her heart began to race. It was time to put it all on the line, but for him. Damn it all if he couldn't give her assurances about love. If she didn't let him in, everything in her life was going to feel as empty as it did right now.

They were on their way to the parking deck when Tara's phone rang. She pulled it out of her purse and saw that it was the main Sterling office number. Normally Grant would call her from his cell, but maybe he'd instead picked up the extension on his desk. "Grant? I'm so glad you called. We have to talk. Right away."

"Ms. Sterling, it's Roz in reception. There's been an accident. It's Mr. Singleton."

Tara's head spun. Her vision went blurry. *No no no no.* This was not happening. She felt queasy. "What happened? Where is he? Please tell me he's alive."

"Yes, he's alive. He was hit by a car."

"Hit by a car?" Her heart plummeted to her stomach.

"He's at the hospital downtown," Roz continued. "If you're still at the presentation, it's only five blocks."

"I'm on my way." Tara hung up and chucked her phone into her bag. "Grant's in the hospital. And I've got to go right now."

"The hospital? What happened?" Astrid seemed just as horrified as Tara was feeling.

"There's no time to explain," Tara blurted.

"I'll drive you." Clay rattled the keys to the van.

"I'll get there faster if I run."

"In heels?" Astrid asked.

"Yes. In heels."

"Should we come with you?" Clay asked.

"Just drive over and meet me there." Tara took off before either of them could argue with her any more. It didn't take long before she realized her shoes were only slowing her down. She took them off and ran in bare feet down the city sidewalks, bobbing between people and trying to see as her eyes clouded with threatening tears.

"If you die, Grant Singleton, I will never, ever forgive you," she said to herself while anxiously waiting for the signal to change at a crosswalk. She darted across as soon as the cars had passed, all the while imagining a life without Grant. It was unthinkable. If she thought she felt empty from doing a presentation without him, what would the rest of her life be like? Her hopes for Sterling would mean nothing without him there. She'd never be able to return without thinking of him, but his absence would haunt her in a way that Johnathon's never had. She and Grant had shared so much in that office. They'd put each other through the wringer. And yet, he was the only person's approval she wanted. He was the one she wanted to share her triumphs with, as well as her failures.

Oh God. He told me he was falling in love with me and I left. Tara couldn't believe she'd done that to him. She hoped against hope that he would be okay when she got to the hospital. He had to be okay, and if he wasn't, she had to hope that he'd be there long enough for her to tell him everything. All of this emotion swelling up inside her had to go somewhere. She couldn't let him go without telling him everything.

As she ran up to the emergency room entrance, the flashbacks started. Johnathon. Her dad. Even her mom. So many people she loved, all gone. She couldn't handle it if it happened again. She simply couldn't go on. Especially if she lost Grant.

She rushed over to the nurses' station. "Grant Singleton?" She could barely get the words out before tears started to stream down her face. This wasn't like her at all. She usually kept it together, especially in a crisis.

The nurse hit a few keys on the computer. "And you are?"

"The woman who loves him and ran in bare feet five blocks to be here for him."

The nurse's mouth pulled into a wide smile. "You need to put those shoes back on before you walk around in the hospital."

"Yeah. Okay." Tara worked her feet back into her shoes. They hurt like hell, but she didn't care.

"He's in room 18. Down the hall, first right, then a left."

Tara was already on her way, but she couldn't sprint here like she had out on the street. Her heart was still pounding and dammit if those tears would not stop. They were running down her cheeks and mascara was staining her blouse. When she got to eighteen, it was one of those big rooms with sliding glass doors. A doctor and several nurses were huddled around him. Tara burst through the door.

"Grant. I'm here. I'm here." She caught sight of his face—the one she loved so much, and something squeezed her heart so tight she could barely stand up. He had bruises and scrapes. One of his amazing eyes was taped shut.

"Tara," he managed, his voice raspy. He even had a tiny smile on his face. Was he delirious?

She pushed one of the nurses out of the way. "I'm sorry. But I have to talk to him." She grabbed his hand and kissed his knuckles, holding them to her lips and drinking in his smell. "You can't die on me. I won't let you."

One of the nurses laughed, which seemed horribly rude.

But then an even bigger smile spread across Grant's lips. "I'm not going to die."

The doctor leaned in. "He's not going to die. He has a concussion and a few broken ribs. That taxi hit him good."

He's not going to die. He's not going to leave me. Tara gasped for air and the tears flowed like a faucet.

"You're crying," Grant said.

"Of course I'm crying." She leaned down and kissed his temple what felt like one hundred times.

"You don't like to cry. You hate it. You never do it."

That was the old Tara he was talking about. Hopefully, she wouldn't return. "I love you. I love you so much and I was an idiot for not seeing it all along."

He managed one more smile, his poor battered face lighting up. "I love you, too, darling."

Oh, thank God. Finally, some relief. She wiped away the tears from her eyes. "You're the best thing in my entire world. I'm resigning from Sterling. I will give you my shares. You can just have them."

"Tara. What about the other wives?"

That seemed to catch the attention of the nurses. They all stopped what they were doing and looked at Tara and Grant.

"It's a long story," Tara said. "I'll tell you when I'm done here." She returned her attention to Grant. "I care about them both, and I hate the idea of breaking promises, but I'll do it. All I want is you."

"Please don't resign. We need you. I need you. You can't leave." Grant pushed back to sit up straighter in bed, but it was clear he was in a lot of pain. Still, he did it. Tara perched on the edge of the bed so she could be closer to him. "Johnathon cut you out of the company in part because he couldn't work with his wife. But I'm not Johnathon."

Tara looked at him as her mind struggled to catch up with his words. "What are you saying?"

"Where's the nurse? She has my clothes."

"Your clothes?" Tara asked.

"They're right here," the nurse answered, handing over a clear plastic bag. Grant's ultraexpensive suit was crammed in there.

He struggled to open it, so Tara helped. "What could possibly be so important that you need to get it out of there?"

"Hold on one minute." He pulled out his suit coat and rummaged around until he found the pocket. He fished a small black box out of it.

Tara's hand flew to her mouth. "No."

"This is not the way I wanted to do this. I was on my way to your presentation when I ducked into the street. The cab came out of nowhere. I wanted to be there for you. I wanted to surprise you."

She pointed at the box. "You were going to give me that afterward?"

"It was so clear on Sunday that you needed convincing. I thought this might help." He popped the box open. Inside was a glimmering diamond solitaire on a slender platinum band. "This isn't the way I planned this. At all. But I'm tired of waiting. Will you marry me?"

Don't wait to be happy. Her dad's words rang through her head like church bells. "Yes, Grant. God, yes. Of course I will." She lowered her head and placed a careful kiss on his lips. She didn't want to hurt him. Not now. Not ever.

He surprised her by gripping her arm and he pulled her closer, then kissed her with such passion that it made her dizzy. When he pulled back, Tara rested her forehead against his.

"That kiss hurt, but it was totally worth it," Grant said.

* * *

Grant stayed in the hospital for three days, which as far as he was concerned was three days too long. He still couldn't believe his big plan to propose to Tara had been ruined in that way, although he had to admit that it paralleled their entire history—rocky, but ultimately solid. She made him so happy by saying yes. It was the sweetest word he'd ever heard, and he'd been waiting an awfully long time to hear it.

Tara brought him back to his house, where he would work from bed for a week until he could return to the office. He wasn't eager to get back to business; he was more eager to feel well enough to make love to Tara and take full advantage of their new status as engaged couple.

"Hey there. How's my handsome patient?" Tara padded into his bedroom with an armful of stuff—a bottle of water, an orange and his laptop. "I figured you would probably want to check email. The whole world has been so worried about you."

Grant took the computer from her and set it aside on the bed. Tara placed the other things on the bedside table. He scooted over and patted the mattress. "Come. Sit. I want to talk."

She delivered a sly grin. "You sure that's all you want to do?"

"I'm working up to that. For now, yes, a conversation."

Tara planted herself on the edge of the bed and

pulled up one leg, intently focused on his face. "Okay. Go."

He laughed and took her hand, bringing her fingers to his lips. "You need to stay at Sterling. I know you said you aren't sure about that part, but if you want to stay, you should. We need you. I need you."

"We haven't heard back from the city yet. They're supposed to announce who made it to the next round today. I keep checking my phone for an answer."

She was missing the point. "I don't care about the city. I mean, I do, because I want this for you, but long term, it doesn't matter. You were always meant to be a driving force at the company and it's my job to make that happen. To restore things to the way they were supposed to be."

"We'd have to figure out how that's going to work. What my real responsibilities would be."

"I think we should be co-CEOs. Run the company together. As equals."

True shock crossed her face. "Oh wow. Do you really think that will work? Won't that ruin your dream of running the ship?"

"Tara. Darling. You are the love of my life. *You* are my dream. Everything with Sterling is gravy. Seriously."

Tara drew in a deep breath, nodding, seeming to process everything he'd said. "I'd get to have the office next to yours?"

"That goes without saying. Whatever you want. You can start picking out furniture as soon as possible."

"And you won't get sick of me? Being with me at work all day and then having to see me at night, too?"

A deep and hearty laugh left his throat. "You have got to be kidding. That sounds amazing."

She smiled and leaned closer, then kissed him softly on the lips. "I love you, Grant Singleton."

"I love you, too." It felt so good to be able to say that. To let the words flow freely from his lips. It felt like he'd waited a lifetime to do that.

Tara's phone beeped with a text. She pulled it out of her pants pocket, then her eyes eagerly scanned it. Her hand flew to her mouth. "It's from Astrid. We made it to the second round." Tara turned her phone around to show him the message.

The happiness he felt for her was so pure, he could hardly stand it. He'd been opposed to the project and now it seemed like the greatest thing in the whole world. Well, maybe after having Tara in his life for real. "That's amazing. I knew you would do it. I knew it."

Tara tapped out an answer. "Astrid will be excited to be working with Clay some more. I think there might be a love connection going on there."

"Oh, geez. I think one office romance is plenty to think about."

"You know…" Tara set down her phone. "We wouldn't even need to get approval from the other shareholders for you and I to be co-CEOs. Between you, me, Astrid and Miranda, that's seventy-one percent. That's more than enough to pass a vote."

"You sure you can keep the other wives in line?"

She nodded, seeming certain of herself. "Astrid is on board, for sure. She's really come into her own in the last few weeks. And Miranda will be ecstatic that we've passed the first hurdle with the Seaport project." Tara gnawed on her finger. "I still need to talk to the city about naming the park after Johnathon. She wants me to work on that."

Grant shook his head and curled his finger to invite Tara closer. "Come here." He didn't want to talk any more about Johnathon or Astrid or Miranda. He didn't want to talk about work. He wanted to enjoy this moment with his future wife. She pressed another soft kiss against his lips.

"We shouldn't start anything, Grant. You're still recovering."

The hell with that. He wrapped his arms around her and pulled her close, then rolled her onto her back. He hovered above her, his ribs aching, but not caring at all about the pain. She was everything he'd ever wanted. And it was time to start their lives together, for real.

Her eyes were wide, her hair splayed across the bed. "Grant. You're injured. What's gotten into you?"

"I love you, Tara. That's what's gotten into me." He lowered his head and whispered in her ear, "And I can't wait to turn you from a Sterling into a Singleton."

* * * * *

Don't miss the next story in
Karen Booth's miniseries, The Sterling Wives:

High Society Secrets

Coming soon from Harlequin Desire!

WE HOPE YOU ENJOYED
THIS BOOK FROM

HARLEQUIN

DESIRE

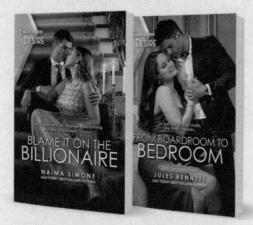

*Luxury, scandal, desire—welcome to
the lives of the American elite.*

Be transported to the worlds of oil barons, family dynasties,
moguls and celebrities. Get ready for juicy plot twists,
delicious sensuality and intriguing scandal.

6 NEW BOOKS AVAILABLE EVERY MONTH!

Available October 6, 2020

#2761 BILLIONAIRE BEHIND THE MASK
Texas Cattleman's Club: Rags to Riches
by Andrea Laurence
A Cinderella makeover for busy chef Lauren Roberts leads to an unforgettable night of passion with a masked stranger—commanding CEO Sutton Wingate. But when the masks come off and startling truths are revealed, can these two find happily-ever-after?

#2762 UNTAMED PASSION
Dynasties: Seven Sins • by Cat Schield
After one mind-blowing night together, bad boy photographer Oliver Lowell never expected to see Sammi Guzman again. Now she's pregnant. Passion has never been their problem, but can this black sheep tame his demons for a future together?

#2763 TEMPTATION AT CHRISTMAS
by Maureen Child
Their divorce papers were never filed! So, Mia Harper tracks down her still-husband, Sam Buchanan, aboard his luxury cruise liner. Two weeks at sea tempts them into a hot holiday affair...or will it become something more?

#2764 HIGH SOCIETY SECRETS
The Sterling Wives • by Karen Booth
Star architect Clay Morgan knows betrayal. Now he keeps his feelings—and beautiful women—at bay. Until he meets his new office manager, Astrid Sterling. Their sizzling chemistry is undeniable, but will a secret from her past destroy everything they've built?

#2765 THE DEVIL'S BARGAIN
Bad Billionaires • by Kira Sinclair
The last person Genevieve Reilly should want is charming jewelry thief Finn DeLuca—even though he's the father of her son. But desire still draws her to him. And when old enemies resurface, maybe Finn is exactly the kind of bad billionaire she needs...

#2766 AFTER HOURS REDEMPTION
404 Sound • by Kianna Alexander
A tempting new music venture reunites songwriter Eden Voss with her ex-boyfriend record-label executive Blaine Woodson. He wronged her in the past, so they vow to keep things strictly business this time. But there is nothing professional about the heat still between them...

---

*A tempting new music venture reunites songwriter
Eden Voss with ex-boyfriend Blaine Woodson, a record
label executive. He wronged her in the past, so they vow
to keep things strictly business this time. But there is
nothing professional about the heat still between them…*

Read on for a sneak peek at
After Hours Redemption *by Kianna Alexander.*

Singing through the opening verse, she could feel the smile
coming over her face. Singing gave her a special kind of joy, a
feeling she didn't get from anything else. There was nothing quite
like opening her mouth and letting her voice soar.

She was rounding the second chorus when she noticed Blaine
standing in the open door to the booth. Surprised, and a bit
embarrassed, she stopped midnote.

His face filled with earnest admiration, he spoke into the
awkward silence. "Please, Eden. Don't stop."

Heat flared in her chest, and she could feel it rising into her
cheeks. "Blaine, I…"

"It's been so long since I've heard you sing." He took a step
closer. "I don't want it to be over yet."

Swallowing her nervousness, she picked up where she'd left
off. Now that he was in the room, the lyrics, about a secret romance
between two people with plenty of baggage, suddenly seemed
much more potent.

And personal.

Suddenly, this song, which she often sang in the shower or
while driving, simply because she found it catchy, became almost
autobiographical. Under the intense, watchful gaze of the man
she'd once loved, every word took on new meaning.

She sang the song to the end, then eased her fingertips away
from the keys.

Blaine burst into applause. "You've still got it, Eden."

"Thank you," she said, her tone softer than she'd intended. She looked away, reeling from the intimacy of the moment. Having him as a spectator to her impassioned singing felt too familiar, too reminiscent of a time she'd fought hard to forget.

"I'm not just gassing you up, either." His tone quiet, almost reverent, he took a few slow steps until he was right next to her. "I hear singing all day, every day. But I've never, ever come across another voice like yours."

She sucked in a breath, and his rich, woodsy cologne flooded her senses, threatening to undo her. Blowing the breath out, she struggled to find words to articulate her feelings. "I appreciate the compliment, Blaine. I really do. But…"

"But what?" He watched her intently. "Is something wrong?"

She tucked in her bottom lip. *How can I tell him that being this close to him ruins my concentration? That I can't focus on my work because all I want to do is climb him like a tree?*

"Eden?"

"I'm fine." She shifted on the stool, angling her face away from him in hopes that she might regain some of her faculties. His physical size, combined with his overt masculine energy, seemed to fill the space around her, making the booth feel even smaller than it actually was.

He reached out, his fingertips brushing lightly over her bare shoulder. "Are you sure?"

She trembled, reacting to the tingling sensation brought on by his electric touch. For a moment, she wanted him to continue, wanted to feel his kiss. Soon, though, common sense took over, and she shook her head. "Yes, Blaine. I'm positive."

Will Eden be able to maintain her resolve?

Don't miss what happens next in…
After Hours Redemption *by Kianna Alexander.*

Available October 2020 wherever
Harlequin Desire books and ebooks are sold.

Harlequin.com